"Who is looking after you?"

He touched her shoulder as gently as she imagined he tended a seedling. Sofia had to fight to keep her focus on what she needed to say.

"You, Sofia." Nathaniel raised his fingers to her cheek. "Who is taking care of *you*?"

Tears burned and Sofia's words deserted her completely.

"I told you from the beginning that I want to help," he continued. "If my presence is helping the boys, I'm glad. Please don't change that on account of me. That's what friends do."

"Do friends do this?" She pressed her hand against his, her crutch slipping away.

"No." Nathaniel framed her face, his eyes continuing to search hers. "Can we not be friends for one minute?"

"I—"

He stopped her. She let her second crutch fall.

Suddenly, he pulled himself away. "I'm sorry. I—"

"Don't behave like this with your friends?" She missed his closeness. The strength she felt from him.

Nathaniel squeezed his eyes shut. "I can't be more than your friend, Sofia…"

Originally from Chicagoland, **Danielle Grandinetti** now lives along Lake Michigan's Wisconsin shoreline with her husband and their two young sons. She is fueled by tea and books and the occasional nature walk. Besides writing for Love Inspired, she also writes historical romantic suspense. Find her online at daniellegrandinetti.com.

Books by Danielle Grandinetti

Love Inspired

A Father for Her Boys

Visit the Author Profile page at LoveInspired.com.

A Father
for Her Boys

Danielle Grandinetti

LOVE INSPIRED
- INSPIRATIONAL ROMANCE

LOVE INSPIRED®

INSPIRATIONAL ROMANCE

ISBN-13: 978-1-335-59833-2

Recycling programs
for this product may
not exist in your area.

A Father for Her Boys

Copyright © 2023 by Danielle Owen

For questions and comments about the quality of this book, please contact us
at CustomerService@Harlequin.com.

Love Inspired
22 Adelaide St. West, 41st Floor
Toronto, Ontario M5H 4E3, Canada
www.LoveInspired.com

Printed in U.S.A.

Behold, I make all things new.
—*Revelation* 21:5

To Gabriel,
my incredible husband
and the amazing father to our boys

Chapter One

❧

Nathaniel Turner wiped the red handkerchief over his grimy face. Sweat, dirt and grass clippings caught in his brown beard and clung to his neck. He stuffed the dirty rag into the pocket of his jeans and lifted his ball cap to pour water from his repurposed milk jug over his head, despite his T-shirt.

That felt better. His tired muscles relaxed, and his head cleared.

He shook off the extra water like his rescue mutt, Dodger, who now lounged in the shade of one of the Allens' gnarly oaks, and surveyed his work. The five acres of freshly cut grass spread out in a gorgeous field. Mr. Allen took pride in keeping his yard pristine, and Nathaniel planned to keep it that way until the older couple returned from helping their pregnant daughter, Cindy. Twins. Nathaniel shook his head. He'd once imagined having kids, but never two at once.

Nathaniel stowed his riding mower in the trailer hitched to the back of his landscaping truck, then whistled for Dodger to follow him toward Mrs. Allen's prized vegetable garden. The woman had won blue ribbons in more categories than anyone else in the last four decades. Her produce, her pickled foods, her pies… Her pies were to die for! She always sent him home with a piece when he came over to help them with any landscaping needs.

Dodger trotted ahead of Nathaniel, tongue hanging from the side of his long snout. The humane society where Nathaniel had gotten Dodger didn't know the dog's breed but suspected he had some pointer based on the brown speckles on his white rump. The rest of him was the same brindle color as the speckles, except for his white, floppy ears and right front foot. Dodger waited for Nathaniel to catch up, and Nathaniel scratched the dog behind the ear.

Mrs. Allen's garden stretched in a hundred-foot by hundred-foot square, and on the far side was a rain reservoir pond—with a fountain in the middle to keep the algae away—that irrigated the garden. Mrs. Allen had collected a substantial harvest of greens and spring veggies before leaving to help her daughter. But, what with it being early summer, Nathaniel would have an ever-growing amount of fruit, vegetables and herbs to harvest every few days. He relished the opportunity, having just a small patio garden outside the back door of his apartment in town. However, these were Mrs. Allen's babies that she raised from seed—no pressure there, even if he was a seasoned landscaper.

Rounding the far edge of the garden, no doubt headed for the pond, Dodger left him to his work. Nathaniel walked the rows, noting what he would need to harvest tomorrow, double-checking the irrigation tubes and looking for weeds. The strawberries and blackberries were just turning ripe. Carrots and rhubarb were in full swing. Not to mention the herbs. And the peas and eggplant were wrapping up until the fall. How did Mrs. Allen think Nathaniel would preserve everything while they were away?

Calculating ideas, he jumped when Dodger let out a howl and raced for the house. Nathaniel frowned. He'd heard the Allens had finally found someone to house-sit for them—someone from Cindy's church near Milwaukee—but the person shouldn't arrive until tomorrow, he thought. He would have offered to house-sit, but that was the one problem with Dodger. Mrs. Allen was allergic to dogs, so Dodger always stayed outside.

Nathaniel followed Dodger around the house. A black sedan was parked in the drive. Dodger sniffed the wheels, until he disappeared around the driver's side. Nathaniel called him back, not wanting the driver to be scared by the over-friendly dog. Dodger obeyed, tail swishing like a windshield wiper. Nathaniel couldn't see the driver clearly, but it appeared to be a dark-haired woman.

Perhaps the house sitter had arrived a day early. Not a problem. It just made him curious. And he'd forgotten to ask the person's name. In fact, he wasn't sure if the person was supposed to be a man or a woman. Mr. Allen had invited him along to a men's event or two with Cindy's church over the years, so perhaps he already knew the person. Then again, people weren't his thing. Plants and dirt were.

Before he could comprehend it, the back doors on either side of the sedan burst open.

"Hey, look, it's a dog!" A boy shouted from the far side of the car.

"A dog?" A boy—Nathaniel guessed him to be seven or so—tumbled from the car as the other boy—apparently of similar age—raced around to join him.

The next instant, the boys stumbled to a halt. Standing side by side, slowly their heads rose to stare at Nathaniel. Nathaniel propped his hands on his hips, studying the pair right back. The boy on the left appeared older than the one on the right simply because he had an extra two inches on him. Both had messy shocks of dark hair and faces full of freckles.

The driver's side door opened. "Rowen. Tucker."

The boys glanced at each other, then darted around him, away from the car. Nathaniel lunged, catching an arm in each hand.

"Hey, let me go!" The older one yanked.

The younger one kicked. "Yeah, mister."

"You need to stay by your mother." Nathaniel pointed the boys back toward the woman who'd emerged from the car as he released them.

"She's not our mom." The older one clamped his arms across his chest, the younger one copying him.

Nathaniel's senses went on alert. Did this woman kidnap these children? Was she planning to hide out in a house she thought was empty?

"She's our aunt," the older one continued, glaring at the car. "And we have to live with her now."

"Yeah. Our mom died." The younger one added.

Oh.

Please God, not now. He couldn't risk anything—especially someone elses' grief—stealing his focus this close to presenting his landscaping bid to the town council. It mattered too much to him. He couldn't fail, not again, not this close to finding his way out of sorrow's darkness.

He refocused on the here and now. Why was the aunt taking so long to get out of the sedan? Was she older? Should he be a gentleman and go help? Maybe corralling the boys would be enough. They seemed ready to take flight again.

Dodger had no qualms about going to investigate the woman. Her quiet voice drifted over as she spoke to the dog. Then she straightened—at least Nathaniel assumed she did. He could only see the mass of black curls she had piled on her head. Another minute and she rounded the front of the car, Dodger at her side.

Definitely not older.

His heart pounded. Dressed in a sleeveless dress covered in yellow sunflowers that stopped at her knees, she looked like summer itself. He hadn't let himself appreciate a woman's beauty since—well, for a long time. And it unnerved him how easily this one could turn his head.

Then he realized she was balanced on two crutches, her left foot in a huge black walking boot.

Nathaniel's distraction allowed the two boys to break free and dart around the house. The woman sighed. He'd offer to go after them after an introduction.

"Is the dog yours?" She scratched behind Dodger's ear despite the crutches. Nathaniel glanced after where the boys ran off to, then back at her.

"He is. I'm Nathaniel Turner." He offered his name in hopes she would do the same, and add the children's names, too.

"Are you taking care of the Allens' yard?" Her eyes darted to his T-shirt with his company logo, then toward his landscaping truck, which had a matching decal on both doors.

"Yup. And you…?" He prompted.

"We're house-sitting." She waved the hand she'd used to pet Dodger toward the Allens' place, then held it out to him. "Sofia Russo, and my nephews are Rowen and Tucker Weston."

"Do you go to Cindy's church?" He wiped his grimy hand on his jeans before he shook hers. It was fragile in his grip, and he took care not to squeeze too hard.

"Yes, and our prayers that her twins stay put have been answered as we hoped so far." Again her glance slipped away from him. "Every day means a better chance for them."

"Are you close friends with Cindy?"

"No. We know each other, but we're not close. I've met her parents a time or two. Our pastor is the one who connected me with her parents about this opportunity. We needed—" She glanced toward the boys, who chose that moment to resurface, looking equal parts ashamed and defiant. "We should get settled."

How he wished she would have finished that sentence. What had she needed? Not that it was his business, nor did he have plans to get invested with anyone, especially a pretty woman, but why had the Allens been willing to let two rambunctious, and disobedient, boys stay in their house without them present?

"Boys, get your things." Sofia popped the trunk with her key fob, the sound moving Nathaniel to action.

"Let me carry your suitcase." He gestured toward her crutches. The question of how she'd become injured hovered on his tongue.

"I've got it." Sofia waved him away even as she took a staggering step.

He grabbed for her arm. "You okay?"

She yanked away, nearly tumbling as her crutches caught on the pavement. "I'm fine. It's completely normal to lose one's balance while managing three legs."

"Sorry. I meant nothing by it." Nathaniel raised his hands in surrender. The boys grabbed a duffel apiece and darted for the front door.

Sofia rubbed the side of her head. "No. I'm sorry. I shouldn't have snapped at you. Gravity is hard on my foot, even if it's not my driving foot. I'll just take my things inside, put on a movie for the boys and rest it."

"Then let me help. I'll grab your things and meet you at the front door." He waggled his hands. "Two strong arms. Don't want to let them go to waste."

A laugh escaped her even as she appeared to tamp down a grin. "Thank you. I suppose that would be the wise thing to do."

He took his time gathering the suitcase, backpack and cloth bag full of books—a rather heavy bag, he had to admit—so he could watch her. She walked slowly, Dodger at her side. She seemed unsteady on her crutches, almost as if she were trying to hide being drunk. But he could tell she wasn't. Anyway, she did not smell of alcohol—though he may have caught the scent of lavender.

Perhaps the crutches were so new she hadn't gotten used to them yet. Or could she be on pain medicine? But she wouldn't have driven her two nephews if she was impaired. Right? Man alive, why was he thinking the worst of her when they'd just met? *Defensive much?* his conscience whispered. *I know, God.*

Insides eating at him, he whistled for Dodger so he wouldn't follow her inside, then instructed the dog to wait on the porch. Dodger cocked his head and sprawled beside the swing, tongue hanging out as he panted.

"There's water in the backyard, Dodge."

The dog glanced at him, closed his mouth then turned back to watching the front yard. Nathaniel shrugged. Dodger knew where to find what he needed and wouldn't leave the yard without him. Anyway, Nathaniel wouldn't be long.

"Sofia?" he called as he entered the Allens' house. No answer. No sound of the boys, either. Worry nipped at his heels. "Sofia!"

The house was an older, two-story home with a modern look. Dark wood floors, white trim and large windows in every room. To the right of the entry was the formal dining room with a glass table and mahogany, high-back chairs. Deeper in the house, their hospitality room, or den, was next to the kitchen, which led to a deck that stretched the width of the house before giving way to the expansive lawn and garden.

Nathaniel bypassed the stairs to the second floor, heading for the den. Pictures of the Allens' children and grandchildren lined the hallway before it opened into the spacious kitchen, with white cabinets and stainless steel appliances. Mrs. Allen liked to cook as much as she liked a spotless kitchen. Nathaniel always wondered how she managed both. He liked to cook, too, but he could never do so without making his kitchen a complete disaster area.

Turning from the kitchen, he went down two steps into the carpeted den. A white brick fireplace surrounded by built-in bookcases, overflowing with books of all sorts, took up the entire far wall. Between it and him was a U-shaped sectional. He spotted her booted foot on the ottoman.

"Sofia?" He left her belongings beside the steps. "Is everything all right?"

"Yes." Her boot disappeared, and her head appeared over the top of the sofa, but she didn't turn toward him. "Sorry. The boys ran upstairs to check out their room, and I saw the bookshelves."

That didn't explain how she ended up on the sofa and the boys nowhere to be heard. Nor why her voice sounded more gravelly than when they were outside. Something was wrong, and he couldn't let it go without making sure she'd be okay.

His muscles tensed, but he kept his tone easygoing as he circled the sofa. "This is my favorite room in the house. Spent many a Saturday afternoon—" He froze at the arm of the sectional as he caught a glimpse of her face. Tears left streaks on her cheeks.

Please God, no. Not now. He couldn't turn away from someone in pain.

His two brothers always ran when they saw a woman crying, even their mom, but when Nathaniel saw tears, it galvanized him into action. Until it burned him. Burned him so bad he kept his secrets close and people far away.

Still. He knew tears were merely the soul releasing emotion, so they'd never scared him. Even nature wept at times. It meant the person needed tending. Care. Like a plant. If he thought of Sofia Russo that way, could he help her without getting hurt? After all, he understood inner pain.

"I know you don't know me, but you can talk to me." He perched on the side of the sectional, kitty-corner to her, but not so close he'd frighten her. He pulled off his ball cap, careful not to spread dirt on Mrs. Allen's furniture. He turned an ear toward the upstairs. Still no sound coming from the boys. Should he offer to go find them first?

"I'm okay." Sofia scrubbed her cheeks and wouldn't meet his gaze. "I'm sorry to make you worry. I should go find the boys."

"Would you prefer I leave?" Nathaniel asked, the question probing more than whether she welcomed his presence.

She hesitated. In fact, she didn't say a word. More importantly, she didn't nod. Of course, she didn't shake her head, either, but he hadn't expected that of her. He was a stranger after all.

"Or I can go after the boys," he offered. He had no idea how she kept up with them on an injured leg. *God, you know how I feel about getting involved with people, so why have you brought this family into my life? Why now?* He bowed his head. How could he not help her? Injured and caring for motherless boys? Talk about kryptonite. *Not my will, Lord, but I'm going to need Your help.*

"I'd appreciate that." She gave a small smile. "I haven't heard anything for several minutes, which never means anything good with them."

"I'm on it. Then I have an idea." He slapped his hands on his thighs, preparing to rise, knowing full well he was about to sacrifice one of his cardinal rules. "You keep studying the books while I wrangle your nephews and fire up the grill. And before you protest, the Allens let me use it all the time. It's way better than the mini one I have at my place. And I know for a fact they left fresh burgers for you because I helped put the groceries away before they left."

She raised her chin.

"I'm over here every few days, and the Allens are like my second family." Nathaniel shrugged, praying that helping Sofia Russo wouldn't hurt him in the end. "I'd like to officially welcome you to their home."

Sofia gently shook her head as she scanned Mrs. Allen's texts. All six of them. The woman had gone on to sing the praises of Nathaniel Turner. Yes, Sofia checked the man's story before agreeing to anything, not that it stopped him from making himself at home. He did seem awful comfortable in the house. Now she understood why. Mrs. Allen considered him the son she never had.

Okay then.

Sofia liked the idea of company, of someone sharing in the relentless task of keeping an eye on her nephews. The fact she willingly allowed a virtual stranger to assist her, no matter what Mrs. Allen said, proved her desperation. And boy howdy, she felt desperate after the drive up from Milwaukee today.

Of course, being unwell always made her feel horribly alone, too, and her foot throbbed like someone had stomped on it. She really could use some pain relief but wouldn't take anything that could dull her ability to care for the boys. They were counting on her, and she couldn't fail them. Not after all they'd lost.

With the boys' latest foray into naughty behavior—they'd been caught trying to shoplift a toy out of the grocery store while she attempted to manage her crutches and the cart last week—her pastor offered her what seemed like a lifesaving opportunity. Take a short leave from her job as his administrative assistant to focus on the boys. Doing so away from their natural habitat, away from the influence of their friends, away from her own responsibilities and in the slower pace of a small town with a yard the size of a city block… Hope sprung for the first time since she'd been asked to identify her sister after a hit-and-run accident left her nephews orphans seven months ago. Their dad had died in service to their country when they were toddlers.

As soon as she'd gotten the house key that morning, she'd packed up the boys and headed north. Only she hadn't anticipated how *hard* it would be. The boys fought her every moment of the trip, and the pain in her foot only added to her distress. So she'd sought refuge before the gorgeous bookcases to find her emotional equilibrium, but it all came crashing down on her. She'd collapsed on the sofa, hoping the handsome landscaper wouldn't notice.

But he had. And he hadn't had a negative reaction. Not like her sister's mother-in-law, who criticized Sofia's parenting at every turn. Or the assistant pastor, who disapproved that she chose to take the boys to a grief counselor instead of using one of the pastors, not that the boys *liked* going there, either. Or her singles group, who didn't understand why she still wept at the most embarrassing times. That's why she'd agreed to Nathaniel's help.

Now she found herself breathing in the incredible scent of charcoal burning and hearing the sounds of the boys playing outside. Her stomach rumbled, and she hobbled to the window. The grill smoked off to the side of the large deck. Beyond, on the lawn, Nathaniel tossed a football with the boys. His dog ran between them as if he could catch it, too. Her heart lurched at the picture it made. At the joy on the boys' faces.

Thank you, God, for Pastor Flores's kindness, for the Allens' generosity. And I pray for Cindy and her babies...

Nathaniel made a diving catch. *And thank you for this handsome landscaper.*

Yes, handsome. The evergreen Turner Landscaping T-shirt he wore showed off the muscles he must have built through his work. The blue baseball hat made him look like the boy next door. However, it was his compassion to her and her nephews that convinced her he was one of the most handsome men she'd ever met. Even when removing his cap showed a line of grime on his forehead and matted brown hair.

An odd excitement hummed through her that she needed to tamp down. She glanced at the texts from Mrs. Allen and smiled. The woman had also made a pointed effort to share the singleness of Nathaniel Turner. Sofia wasn't looking for a boyfriend—she could barely manage the two boys God had placed in her life—but knowing she didn't have to worry about a jealous girlfriend made Sofia rest easier about spending a couple hours with him as a friend.

The sliding of the patio door alerted her to Nathaniel's return. She turned from the window. "It smells delicious."

"Good!" Nathaniel had an easy smile to go with his hearty voice. She liked how it made her feel, especially right now when her world was so topsy-turvy.

"What can I do to help?"

"Tell me whether or not you like cheese on your hamburger." Nathaniel's head disappeared into the massive refrigerator. "They've got cheddar—both mild and sharp—Swiss, pepper jack, provolone, American...probably a few others if I can find them."

"I suppose we are in the heart of dairy country."

Nathaniel peered around the refrigerator door. "It's all Wisconsin-made, too. There's a cheese factory not far from here that sells their cheese in a small storefront."

She did love local shops. "I'll have mild cheddar. The boys, too."

"Good choice." Nathaniel reached into the fridge again, then popped out with an exuberant expression. "Aha! Mrs. A left a bag of cheese curds!"

Sofia laughed. "Why are cheese curds so momentous?" She got them all the time for her nephews.

Nathaniel waved the bag. "Because I ran out two days ago and haven't gotten to the store yet. And these are the best kind."

"Duly noted. The way to make Nathaniel Turner's day is cheese curds."

"This kind in particular." He crossed over to her and opened the bag. "Try one."

She popped the blob of cheese in her mouth and bit down. It squeaked like a proper cheese curd, and the sharp flavor burst over her tongue. "You're right. I haven't found curds this good in Milwaukee."

"See?" He held out the bag again.

She nodded as she took one, but a cry from outside had her dropping it back into the bag so she could grip her crutches. Nathaniel tossed the bag onto the counter as he dashed outside ahead of her.

Chapter Two

"Do we need to call 911?" Sofia called after Nathaniel as he took the deck steps in one bound, his heart galloping ahead of him.

Dodger sniffed Tucker's face as he lay on his back in the middle of the yard. Fresh-cut grass covered his clothes. No blood gushed, no bones stuck out or limbs faced the wrong direction. The boy's eyes were open, too.

Nathaniel knelt beside him. What did he know about children's injuries?

"I didn't mean anything by it." Rowen stood at his elbow, arms crossed, obviously attempting to appear defiant or aloof, but Nathaniel spotted the fear in his eyes. The same fear he felt. That he was somehow at fault.

Tucker's pale face revealed a multitude of freckles. "I can't breathe."

Nathaniel pulled up Dr. Bradley's number as Sofia managed to cross the soft lawn. Worry deepened the lines around her mouth, and she stumbled. Nathaniel jumped to help her, noting the tears that swam in her eyes, as Dr. Bradley answered his phone.

Nathaniel eased Sofia down to her knees. "Hi, Dr. Bradley. It's Nathaniel… Yeah, I'm over at the Allens'. Their house sitter's nephew tumbled and said he's having a hard time breathing."

"Is he turning blue around the lips or fingernails?" Dr. Bradley's calm voice slowed Nathaniel's heart rate.

"No, sir, not that I can tell."

"Good. I'll be there in two minutes."

Nathaniel let out a breath. "Dr. Bradley is a primary care and family medicine doc who lives about five houses thataway." He pointed his chin over Sofia's shoulder and rested a hand on Tucker's arm, a sense of responsibility washing over him for the motherless boy. "You hang in there."

Tucker nodded.

"What happened?" Sofia turned into the breeze to blow a fallen curl out of her face. She reached a hand for her older nephew. "Can you tell me, Ro?"

Neither boy said a word. Tucker kept his gaze averted, and Rowen toed the ground.

"Boys." The warning in Sofia's voice caused Rowen's back to straighten.

Nathaniel bit his tongue to keep from stepping into the middle of her parenting. Instead, he opted for squeezing her shoulder, hoping Sofia would take comfort from his presence. She closed her eyes at his touch. They'd come here to heal, and he sensed they all needed this first night to go well.

"He ran for the ball, tripped and landed flat on his back." Rowen slammed his toe into the ground. "I didn't mean nothin' by it. We were just playing catch. Is he going to die now, too?"

Nathaniel's heart broke, and he fought to keep from adding his own tears to those running down Sofia's cheeks. Two tears escaped Tucker's eyes, too.

"No one is going to die." Sofia grabbed her nephews by the hand. "You hear me? The doctor will be here any minute, and he'll make sure Tuck is just fine."

Dodger alerted them to Dr. Bradley's arrival a moment later. Nathaniel couldn't help but be grateful not to talk more about death. It carved up his insides enough. To know these boys had dealt with it, too…it made him care about them even as it tore him apart.

Nathaniel made introductions, then invited Rowen to help him with the hamburgers, which were probably going to be charred to the point of being inedible. He remembered being Rowen's age, caught between an older brother and a young one. Nathaniel didn't want to get close to people anymore, but surely he could connect with a kid when they had the loss of a loved one in common.

Rowen followed, dragging his feet, until Nathaniel gave Dodger a signal to stay by the boy's side. Rowen set his hand on the dog's back, and Dodger led him to the deck. Dodger understood grief, too.

"What do you know about grilling, Rowen?" Nathaniel lifted the grill lid, releasing a cloud of smoke into the sky. Nathaniel attempted to send his emotion with it. He needed to push aside his memories for the sake of the boy.

"My dad grilled. Before." Rowen shrugged. "My grandpa doesn't like to, though."

"Your mom's dad or your dad's dad?" The burgers were definitely well-done. He grabbed the serving plate and quickly removed the patties from the grill. They weren't blackened nor were they stiff to the point of being dried out. There was hope in that.

Nathaniel brought the plate with him as he went inside so Dodger wouldn't get them.

"My dad's dad. Mom and Aunt Sofi don't have a dad. Or a mom." Rowen followed. Dodger stayed, knowing his boundary line.

Nathaniel held out the cheese curds, unsure what to say.

Rowen took one. "Do you have a dad?"

"I do." Nathaniel set the plate of hamburgers on the counter and pulled out the cheese slices. Usually he put them on while the patties were still on the grill, but he didn't want to leave them over the flame any longer. "His name is Paul Turner. Maybe you'll get to meet him while you're here. He lives just outside town."

"I miss having a dad."

What was he supposed to say to that? His parents were alive and well. Thoughts of April pushed into his mind like a painful thorn. Okay, yes, he had plenty in common with Sofia and her nephews, but that wasn't something he planned to share with anyone.

"Will Tucker really be okay?" Rowen rocked a kitchen chair.

Nathaniel left the food on the counter and

knelt in front of Rowen. "I know Dr. Bradley took good care of me when I was your age. I broke bones, sprained ankles and cut myself on stuff all the time because I played outside so much. Now look at me. So I know Tucker is in the best hands, and I'm sure he'll be just fine."

Rowen blinked and nodded. "Thanks, Mr. Nate." The boy turned on his heel, disappearing outside, Dodger on his heels.

His heart turning in his chest, Nathaniel watched Rowen jump down the steps. *Why now, Lord?*

Sofia breathed a sigh of relief. The kind Dr. Bradley assured her Tucker merely had the wind knocked out of him. A common boyhood trouble when playing hard—and her nephews surely did that. Nobody's fault. Nothing to worry about. In fact, Tucker had already leaped to his feet and retrieved the football they'd been tossing around. Rowen and Dodger met him, and the game commenced again.

"I can't thank you enough," she told the doctor as he helped her stand and situate her crutches under her arms. "How much do I owe you for coming over?"

Dr. Bradley waved her off. Gray-haired, bespectacled and clean-shaven, he reminded her of an old Dick Van Dyke. "House calls like this are no charge. I'm sure I'll be over again before you're through house-sitting."

That made Sofia's stomach turn.

"How long have you had the boys?" His question was quiet but pointed. Sofia tried not to react negatively or defensively, yet she prepared for his criticism about her taking on the care of two boys as a single, working woman. As her mother-in-law constantly reminded her.

"Seven months now. My sister died just before Thanksgiving." Her memories dragged her back to the phone call that had had her running to the hospital. Arriving just in time to say goodbye. The funeral. The holidays. The lawyers and arguments and finally the decision that Anna Weston's final wishes be granted.

"I'm glad the Allens set you up here. This is a good community for kids. Fresh air. Open land. And—" Dr. Bradley leaned closer "—I recommend trusting Nathaniel. He's good people. You can feel safe around him. Your boys, too."

Sofia blinked away those ever-ready tears.

She'd sensed the truth to Dr. Bradley's words, but to hear the old doctor express it so clearly erased any anxiety she had left over the matter. It also chipped at the wall that protected her heart, and that would never do. Not to mention, she couldn't let someone into their family who would only be a temporary presence, since they would return home before the summer ended. They'd come here to heal, not make matters worse.

"And the foot?" Dr. Bradley pointed to her black boot.

"A stress fracture." From missing her step on the Fourth of July parade float frame she'd pulled out of storage last week. She'd been hurrying to finish in time to pick up the boys from their last day of school. Pastor Flores had had to drop her off at the hospital while he picked up the boys. Another epic failure on her record.

"Have your doctor send me your file, and I can manage your check-ups. No need to drive all the way back to Milwaukee just to monitor it." Dr. Bradley held out a hand again. "It was a pleasure to meet you, Sofia. Stay off that foot, and you let me know if you need anything, all right?"

She stared at him for a minute before her

thoughts caught up enough to make her mouth work. "Thank you, Dr. Bradley. That's very kind of you." No criticism, simply an offer of help. Like Pastor Flores. And the Allens. *And Nathaniel?*

"Aunt Sofi!" Tucker hollered. Obviously he was breathing fine at that volume. "Time to eat!"

Dr. Bradley chuckled, winked at Sofia then waved to the boys. "You two listen to your aunt!"

The next afternoon, Nathaniel parked his truck beside the Allens' front curb. He tapped the steering wheel, embarrassment pinning him in place. He'd actually stopped at home to change into fresh clothes before coming over to complete the last job of his day. He only did that when he wanted to make a good impression on a potential customer. Today's motivation had nothing to do with customer service, and he knew it. He'd stayed up half the night, his mind alternating from the heartache in Rowen's eyes, which echoed his own, the fear from Tucker's fall that brought back way too many memories, and... Sofia Russo.

Verses from James 2 came back to him in the night like a judge. How could he wish

Sofia well and do nothing? How could he hope the boys would mind her without offering a hand? ... *Faith, if it hath not works, is dead*... Over and over the phrase pounded, forcing him to face his fear of getting close to someone or risk disobeying God.

In his sleeplessness, he'd read over Mrs. A's texts again. Sofia sounded amazing—a reason to stay away, in all honesty. Though Mrs. Allen had only met her a few times, apparently, Sofia's reputation spoke volumes. As the church admin person, Sofia interacted with many people, and not one of Cindy's hospital visitors had a negative word about her. However, each one had expressed concern about her since she'd taken on the care of her nephews.

This morning, Nathaniel replied to Mrs. Allen's text, specifically asking more about what she meant by that. He needed to know why they were concerned, to better understand what he'd be walking into if he decided to follow God's prompting and offer his help.

Mrs. A had replied immediately.

Stop fretting. Sofia is not a complication. She's beautiful.

Her nephews are grieving and pushing their

boundaries. They got caught shoplifting. It's why she's there.

Help her, Nate. Or at least offer your support. It'd be good for both of you.

Her reply overcame his battle with God and sent him looking for a dinner invitation... again.

"Mr. Nate!" Rowen smashed into his driver's side door, hands splayed beside the face he pressed against the glass.

Dodger barked from the back seat of the cab, his tail whacking Nathaniel in the head.

"Dodger!" Tucker jumped up and down beside Rowen. "Can I let him out? Aunt Sofi said I had to ask first."

Smart woman. Nathaniel opened his door and gave permission for Dodger to be loosed. Before he rounded the front of his truck, Dodger and the boys were racing for the backyard. Sofia stood on the front porch with her eyes shaded by her hand and crutches tucked under her arms.

He waved and made his way toward her. "I hope you don't mind me stopping by unannounced."

"What brings you?" She adjusted her balance with the crutches.

"I need to look over the garden." Nathaniel picked up his pace. How honest should he be? The garden wasn't a ruse, but it did mask his motives.

"I found lemonade in the fridge. Would you like a glass?"

"Absolutely. Mrs. A's lemonade is legendary." Nathaniel held the screen door for her while she maneuvered inside.

Sofia chuckled. She seemed in much better spirits today. Maybe he didn't need to stay. Then again, what else would he do tonight but pore over his presentation for the millionth time. Perhaps the distraction would actually be beneficial.

Tomorrow he would present his plan for refurbishing the Town Circle, a community green space at the heart of River Cove. All bids would be presented throughout the day tomorrow—Saturday—and then the council would vote in a closed-door meeting on Monday night. His future dreams, and past promises, depended on their decision. Not to mention, getting the Town Circle contract would open doors for his landscaping company that would potentially allow him to expand and grow. And maybe find healing.

...Faith, if it hath not works, is dead...

Right. And pure religion cared for the fatherless. How could he desire to do the right thing before God and be so afraid of the risk at the same time?

Sofia juggled her crutches as she retrieved four glasses and poured the lemonade. She seemed so determined to accomplish the task, despite the crutches getting in her way, that Nathaniel kept his hands clasped behind his back to keep from jumping in prematurely.

"Would you mind carrying these to the deck?" Sofia glanced at him with a twinkle in her brown eyes. "I know you're dying there, not offering to help."

A laugh escaped. "You caught me."

She raised an eyebrow. "Is that the real reason you're here? To offer help?"

Nathaniel drummed his fingers on the counter, again debating what to say.

She pursed her lips. "Did Mrs. Allen put you up to this?"

"Something she said contributed."

Sofia cringed.

"You probably already know how anxious the people back at your church are for you. It sounds like the boys are a…handful." He hesitated, hoping he didn't overstep.

Without replying, Sofia led the way outside, carefully navigating the deck with her crutches. She looked gorgeous in the deep green T-shirt and light-wash jeans she wore. Like she belonged in a forest garden with an old stone house, hand-built fireplace, and—he stopped himself.

He'd made the mistake of mentioning to Mrs. Allen that he'd grilled the hamburgers she'd left in the fridge last night, and her texts were messing with Nathaniel's head. This was not meant as a date. No, Nathaniel was here on a selfless mission to help. He'd show the compassion of Jesus, then be on his way. No heartache involved.

"Both our pastor and the boys' counselor think acting out is their way of expressing grief." Sofia brought him out of his thoughts. "Which is why both thought coming out here would be such a good idea. I think they're right. In the twenty-four hours we've been here, they've been outside every waking minute. I've never heard them laugh as much as they have since Anna…" Her voice hitched and she fell silent.

"And what about you, Sofia?" Nathaniel set down the glasses on the table, praying he wasn't messing up by asking the question that had been nagging him since he'd heard about the boys' troubles. He agreed with the pastor and counselor that being here would likely help the boys, but Sofia needed care, too, for both her foot and her grief.

"What about me?" Sofia stopped in the middle of the deck with a confused expression.

"Have you laughed since it happened?" How else could he word it? He still struggled to find lightheartedness, and it had been three years. For her, she'd lost her sister not even a year ago and had to care for her grieving nephews while managing her own sorrow. Nathaniel couldn't imagine it.

She ducked her chin. "Sounds like you know something of it."

"I understand losing something close to you. Having a dream taken away without warning." He shifted, skirting around the truth. This wasn't about him, and he wouldn't talk about April.

Sofia stayed quiet. After a sip of lemonade, she maneuvered over to the deck railing.

Nathaniel joined her but kept his focus out across the yard in front of them, where the boys played with Dodger. His heart hammered. He was playing with fire, asking these types of questions. Mrs. Allen may think she excelled at being a matchmaker, but that didn't mean Sofia's heart was available. Nathaniel's certainly wasn't.

"Nathaniel, I would be remiss if I didn't say thank-you for your help yesterday. And the boys sure are enjoying running after Dodger. Though I'm afraid we've infringed on your time. Surely you have better things to do than return again today after spending the evening with us yesterday."

Nathaniel shrugged. "I always save the Allens' house for last, and an empty apartment is all that's waiting for me." Why did he say all that, even if it was the truth? This was about Sofia, not him. "Can I get you anything else? Maybe ice for your foot?"

She opened her mouth to protest, he was sure of it, so he held up a hand to stop her.

"Remember I have two functioning legs and those two strong arms I happened to mention yesterday. Let me help." And then he needed to get out to the blackberry brambles before he made a fool of himself.

"But you won't be with us when we return home." Red the color of a vibrant peony spread across her entire face. "I don't mean to hurt your feelings or sound ungrateful. I'm incredibly thankful. It's just these boys and me. We have to find a way through this together. You understand, don't you?"

"Of course." Was this God letting him off the hook?

"I'm glad you think so. I have to have my nephews' best interests at the forefront of everything I decide."

He set his elbows on the deck railing and his arm brushed Sofia's, making him extra aware of her. "What about your foot?"

Sofia's shoulders slumped.

Which is probably why he blurted out, "What if we helped each other?" before he thought it all through.

Sofia eyed him. "What do you mean?"

"See, I have a little problem myself." He flashed her a smile to hide the churning in his mind as it scrambled to catch up with his mouth. "Tomorrow I share my proposal for the Town Circle renewal project. The Circle is our community green space. It is in great need of a facelift, and as a local landscaper, I want that opportunity. It would be a benefit to everyone, including me."

"But?" She tilted her head.

"But some have pushed back at having the Circle updated. I just didn't expect it to continue after the town voted in favor of it last week. One of the more influential members of the community confronted me about the project this morning, and it has me…nervous for what she could do to stop the project."

"A project you need if you want to grow your business?"

If only it were that simple. "I want to address her concerns in my proposal."

"Which will show how well you listen to the community and will, perhaps, help your bid."

"It sounds mercenary if you put it that way, but I also care about the project." More than he wanted to share right now. "Would you be willing to listen to my proposal and give suggestions on what I could adjust?"

She rested cold fingers on his arm. "All you want is a sounding board? No strings attached?"

"It's that simple." He took her hands and rubbed warmth back into them.

She watched his movements, and he immediately let go. "But you said we could help one another. How do you want to help me?"

"I want to help you while you're here in River Cove and laid up with that foot. So let's say you can call in your favor at any point while you're here this summer." He wanted to add *or afterward*, but he wasn't about to commit either of them to a friendship past these next several weeks.

A tear splashed down her cheek.

His heart twisted. He hadn't set out to make her cry. "Is that not what you wanted? Did I say something wrong? I didn't mean—"

She shook her head. "It's one of the sweetest things anyone has done for me since Anna. And we'd just be friends? No ulterior relationship like it seems Mrs. Allen is trying to promote?"

"Not at all. None. I promise that has nothing to do with this." How could it when Nathaniel's own heart would never allow him to get close enough to a woman to have that type of relationship? Friendship pushed his limits, but he couldn't just desert Sofia and her nephews, not after hearing how grief had them tangled in its web.

"And you'd really do that for me?"

"Don't make me sound better than I am," Nathaniel mumbled, his conscience poking at him for needing a cattle prod just to show up this afternoon. "I am asking for a favor in advance."

She laughed as she used her shoulder to swipe her tears away. "Hardly a fair trade-off."

He smiled, keeping his thoughts to himself. Because seeing her happy, that made his offer worth it. Of course he wouldn't tell her that, especially since he'd promised her friendship. Anything more and his own panic would set in. He couldn't do that to her when she needed support. He meant to help her, and anything he got out of it was merely extra.

"Maybe we should call the boys to join us for lemonade." Sofia nodded toward the table.

Point taken. They needed to move on from their deep conversation.

His phone dinged before either of them could holler for Sofia's nephews. His pulse sped up until he realized he'd received another text from Mrs. Allen, going out of her way to encourage him to be nice to Sofia— she knew his struggle not to be a loner since April's death, but nothing more.

He shook his head. This budding personal connection felt more like a noose. With a pat to the deck railing, he escaped inside. He stopped in the middle of the kitchen floor, searching for a reason to give Sofia when she asked why he'd gone inside. Her foot!

In no time, he had her set up on the lounge chair on the deck, her leg free of the boot and an ice pack resting on her ankle. The boys guzzled their lemonade, then he grabbed the basket Mrs. Allen used for gathering and headed out to the garden with her shears.

The boys joined him, eating half the blackberries they picked. They told him about the sports they played before their mom died, the cool house they used to live in and how Aunt Sofi would visit every Friday for ice cream. He made a mental note to purchase ice cream for next Friday night.

Berries gathered, he scanned through the rest of the garden. He found one squash ready and the last of the asparagus. It gave him an idea for dinner, a way he could help Sofia without forging a deeper connection with her. The boys appeared skeptical with his plan, but they followed him as he picked the herbs he'd need for seasoning. He took the time to point out weeds, too, tossing them aside as they walked the rows.

Sofia's eyes were closed when he returned to the deck, so he went inside to see what meat options Mrs. Allen had left in the refrigerator, happy to see the stir fry beef he'd remembered from helping her unpack the groceries.

The boys tossed the football on the lawn while Nathaniel watched them from the kitchen window. It felt entirely too domestic, as if they were his boys. His hands shook as he chopped the vegetables, and he set down the knife with a whoosh of air.

He and April had wanted multiple kids, but after her death, he'd pushed the idea of family away. How could he ever hope to have one when he had no desire to risk his heart again? Now, following through on his promise to help Sofia meant facing his past head-on. As long as he kept reminding himself he'd never be a father for her boys.

Chapter Three

Sofia woke to an aching foot and the sound of her nephews happily shouting. A ball sailed across the sky, and a dog barked. She sat up in time to see Tucker leap into the air to catch the ball in the stomach before tumbling to the ground.

And that's how he got hurt yesterday.

Ugh. Gone was cool Auntie Sofi. She was an annoying mom now. Pain pierced her heart. She could never replace Anna. Didn't want to.

Before she had the chance to remind the boys to be careful, her nose registered a smell that had her stomach rumbling. Garlic and onions, plus other spices she couldn't put her finger on. Was Nathaniel cooking again? The shade stretched into the yard, and a cool breeze caused goose bumps to rise. How long had she slept?

She secured the boot around her bad leg, then grabbed her crutches and pushed to her good foot. Holding onto one of the crutches with her elbow, she slid the patio door open. Nathaniel stood at the stove, his broad back stretching the fabric of his work T-shirt, his baseball cap on backward. Shorts today instead of jeans, and green-stained gym shoes.

He turned toward her.

"What smells so good?"

"Stir fry." He shrugged, as if nervous to be caught cooking. Frankly, it was incredibly attractive. Way too attractive, in fact, especially after she basically told him she couldn't risk the boys getting attached to him. Herself, either.

Of course, then he'd gone on to make a deal that melted her heart. She didn't doubt that's why she'd rested better than she had since she first broke her foot. It left her feeling as emotionally unsteady as her three-legged balance.

And now she needed to remind him they couldn't get used to him being here like this. It was the only way to keep from getting attached to him. "I can make dinner, Nathaniel."

No response.

She swung her crutches until she stood by his side. Strong and trustworthy. She'd like to rely on him, and her resolve to send him away wavered. "Nathaniel?"

"I want to help, Sofia."

The way he said it, the amount of sincerity, almost as if she were doing *him* the favor by letting him cook dinner…it moved her. She was used to being the one serving others. Her job saw to that. Coordinating, facilitating, getting coffee, water, snacks and anything anyone needed for meetings, for speakers and for charity events. She served the servers. And she loved her job.

But the past few months, she'd been drained. Then she'd injured her foot, and her most treasured project, the Fourth of July float, had been handed off to a random volunteer. She pushed the disappointment of that away because her nephews came first. Caring for them had to be her priority. It was why she was here in River Cove.

Then Nathaniel entered their lives. He radiated quiet determination. As if he'd made it his mission to take care of *her*. She had plenty of people who wanted to help. Nathaniel did, too. But she sensed his motivation centered on her, and it simultaneously caused gratitude to wash through her and butterflies to swarm inside.

"If you send your nephews in, I'll have them set the table outside and we can eat."

"Sure." She laughed because she had yet to get the boys to do any such thing, no matter how much she begged, scolded, punished or asked nicely. It was a daily irritation because she knew they set the table every day for Anna. Sliding open the patio door, she called out her instructions. No response, and her shoulders sagged.

Nathaniel appeared behind her, a solid presence against her back. "Mind if I try?"

She shrugged because he might as well.

"Boys!" His voice reverberated through her. "What did your aunt say?"

Rowen and Tucker froze, the football thudding to the ground at Rowen's feet. Nathaniel gave her a gentle nudge with his elbow and walked away.

She watched him return to the stove before collecting herself. "Time to set the table!"

The boys looked at one another, then ran up the deck steps to obey. Sofia stepped aside, dumbfounded.

As the boys reached the island where Nathaniel stacked the plates and silverware, he stopped them. "Why didn't you listen to your aunt?"

Red climbed the cheeks of both boys, but Sofia held herself back from intervening.

"Make sure everyone has water, and one of you help your aunt out to the table."

The boys scrambled to do exactly what Nathaniel instructed, and in moments, Sofia found herself sitting down as the three of them served her before joining her for dinner. As Nathaniel offered to pray and insisted they join hands, Sofia set hers in his and squeezed. Nathaniel kept his head bowed, so she squeezed again, and he finally glanced at her.

Thank you, she mouthed.

Nathaniel squeezed back and prayed for dinner.

"You dig up our Town Circle and I'll see you never get another bid in this town ever again." Mrs. Reynolds stood toe-to-toe with Nathaniel in the Town Hall, her fiery eyes showing a distinct lack of intimidation though she stood nearly two feet shorter than him.

"Mrs. Reynolds, the mayor—"

"That upstart?" The older woman jabbed

her crooked finger into his stomach. "He doesn't know anything."

Nathaniel rested his hands on his belt. Five minutes until his presentation, and Mrs. Reynolds had him cornered. Whether she singled him out or whether she also confronted the other three landscapers, Nathaniel didn't know. But right now, he felt a noose tightening around his neck. Or maybe it was his tie. He definitely needed air. Away from Mrs. Reynolds.

"It's been a green space for as long as I remember," Mrs. Reynolds continued on with information Nathaniel already knew. "We had first kisses and took wedding pictures on that lawn. We've worked hard to maintain the grass and keep it from getting muddy. Now you want to dig it up!"

He knew it would do no good to reiterate the fact that the town already voted to refurbish the Town Circle. It would get dug up, by him or someone else. Today wasn't about whether to landscape the Town Circle. It was about *who* would do the digging. And he wanted to be that person, more than anyone knew.

"Mrs. Reynolds." Nathaniel kept his voice calm in hopes he'd get through to her. "If

I'm awarded the bid, you can trust that I will honor that space. People will still be able to take pictures and have—" he cleared his throat as a knife sliced his heart "—first kisses." His own first kiss had been there, too. With April.

"But it won't be the same." Mrs. Reynolds deflated, looking more like a little old church lady in her dress and pearls.

Compassion rose up. "No, Mrs. Reynolds, it won't be the same. I hope to make it better. Come inside and listen to my ideas. I plan to lay out my design for the space. Then later, you can voice any concerns during—"

"If you don't remove your bid—" Mrs. Reynolds nearly vibrated with her anger "—then be prepared to lose everything."

His jaw dropped as the diminutive woman stormed off. What had a bee in her bonnet? If he won the bid, then he'd best not underestimate her, which meant he'd better find out why she was so all-fired determined to have him remove his bid. Was it him, or was it the land? Or was it something else entirely? And how was he going to find the answer?

"She sure was mad." A boy's voice brought Nathaniel around. Leave it to Tucker to state the obvious.

Sofia turned her chin into her shoulder, but Nathaniel didn't miss her grin. She wore a blue dress with a field of white daisies. It covered her black boot, but her crutches and off-kilter stance told him she still wore it.

"Does that mean you aren't talking in front of everyone or whatever it is you're doing?" Rowen shrugged as if he didn't care, but Nathaniel didn't miss the weight behind the question. For some reason, this mattered to the boy, and Nathaniel didn't want to let him down.

"I'm still presenting my bid." Nathaniel rested a hand on Rowen's shoulder. "I hope I can answer Mrs. Reynolds's questions, but I can only take one step at a time. I sure am glad to see all of you, though." He met Sofia's eyes. "This is a surprise." More welcome than Nathaniel would have guessed.

"We wanted to hear your speech." Tucker looked up at him, like he could do anything. "Aunt Sofi said it would be about plants, like you were telling us about yesterday."

As the daylight faded, he'd shared his proposal with Sofia. She'd prompted him to strengthen areas and reword sections. Most of all, she'd encouraged him not to limp by with surface reasons for why he wanted this bid.

Nathaniel swallowed the emotion in his throat. Could he open up enough?

His parents and brothers were here and already seated. Other townspeople who he knew supported him were also here, too. But having Sofia and her nephews here to cheer him on? It meant more than he could find the words to express, and he had no idea why.

"They're ready for you, Nate," Mayor Keller called from the doorway to the hall.

"You've got this." Sofia's quiet confidence bolstered his, and he strode to the podium, prepared to lay his dreams at the feet of his neighbors.

Sofia sat between her nephews in the back row of the hall. The people who packed the room quickly quieted down when the mayor introduced Nathaniel.

He stepped to the podium and scanned the crowd, nodding to a few people, before his eyes found hers. He wore a long-sleeve dress shirt that bore his company's logo, a burgundy tie and black slacks. It gave him a professional look that should serve him well.

Lord, please give him the right words.

She was nervous for him. When he'd practiced on her last night after dinner, she could sense this project mattered to him more than he would admit. She tried to help him express how much he cared, but he'd held back. Would he show his passion in the presentation? She had no doubt Nathaniel knew his flowers, but that's not what impressed her. He loved his town.

"We all have memories of the Town Circle," Nathaniel began.

He clicked a button, causing a picture to appear on the screen behind him. It showed a plain, albeit massive, green space, enclosed by a cement curb. Outside one quarter of the circle was a parking lot. Another picture appeared, showing a wooden sign with the name Town Circle.

"Every community picnic, festival and parade centers around this space. Kids gather after school. Those of you who've seen a few more summers than a youngster like me—" chuckles rippled through the audience "—still sit on the benches to watch the wildlife."

Nathaniel looked around the room, his gaze once again connecting with Sofia's. She nodded her encouragement. It was the least she could do. In the two evenings he'd spent with them, he'd lifted some of the weight from her shoulders. Even her foot ached less today, and she couldn't help but think he had something to do with it. Not to mention, her nephews hadn't stopped talking about him all day. Who knew they'd actually be excited to go to a town hall meeting?

"It's looked the same way for as long as I remember," Nathaniel continued on, sharing a story about a summer relay race and a Christmas nativity. "These stories are what make up the Town Circle, and I have no intention of disrupting or destroying the heart of our town."

Our. Sofia warmed. It was more than a good business move, which is how he'd presented it to her at first. She'd pushed back, getting him to tell her stories about his time on the Town Circle. His eyes had glazed with memory. So she'd told him he needed to show a piece of his heart by using inclusive language. And he listened!

"I'm a homegrown River Cove boy. I grew up here, and my youngest memories center around the Town Circle."

Nathaniel looked off to the side, as if distracted by one of those memories. Sofia scrunched the fabric of her skirt in her fist, praying he'd stay on track.

With a shake of the head, Nathaniel clicked

to a computerized design. "My vision for our Town Circle involves adding depth and color to the space we already love. If I receive the bid to refurbish our Town Circle, my goal is to be finished before the Fourth of July Celebration."

Sofia blinked back unwelcome tears. She knew Nathaniel's deadline—he'd told her last night—so it shouldn't have made her emotional. But July Fourth was her and Anna's favorite holiday. It was *their* holiday. And this would be the first year they wouldn't be able to celebrate together. Nevertheless, she had to set aside those emotions to make the holiday special for Anna's boys. They were now her priority.

Monday night, Nathaniel joined Sofia and her nephews for dinner at Sofia's invitation. When she asked him to help her in the kitchen afterward, he realized what she was doing. She knew the council vote was tonight and was doing her best to keep his mind off it.

"You don't have to do this," he insisted as he put dishes in the dishwasher. She'd made baked mac and cheese, which they'd devoured.

"Do what?" Sofia shrugged as she called

the boys in from outside. They'd lingered over dinner until the boys' bedtime. "You don't have plans already, do you?"

The hope in her voice had Nathaniel rubbing his scruff. His plan had been to pace his small apartment until his phone rang with the council's decision. Being here was a pleasant distraction for him.

"Then please stay." Sofia watched the boys make their way toward the house. He noticed they'd been listening better since he'd challenged them. "I don't get much adult conversation being here, and I didn't realize how much I'd miss it."

The patio door slid open, and two Tasmanian devils whirled into the room.

"Say good-night to Nathaniel, then go upstairs to wash up before getting into bed." The boys whined, but it all seemed centered around him leaving rather than not being tired for bed—if he interpreted their grumbling right.

"I'll be back tomorrow to harvest more from the garden." Nathaniel offered high fives.

The boys brightened considerably and scrambled upstairs louder than before.

"They look up to you." Sofia kept her gaze on where her nephews had disappeared.

There was something in her voice that pulled at him. Before he could discern what that something was, he agreed to be here once she got the boys settled. She turned to him, then, with a smile that made his heart stutter. The genuineness made her eyes shine, as if he were doing *her* the favor by spending the evening with her. No teasing or flirting or flinging herself at him. Just joy at his presence. And then she was gone, up the stairs, to put her nephews to bed.

He mulled over her reaction as he finished loading the dishwasher and taking out the trash. He puttered around the lower level, making sure light bulbs worked and nothing needed fixing. Still, he couldn't get her expression out of his head. He'd withdrawn since he lost April, and he wasn't ready to offer himself again. Yet here he was and willing to stay.

He gathered an ice pack from the freezer, tossing it over his shoulder as he carried two glasses of lemonade outside. Dodger met him at the door and followed him as he set them on the short table nestled between the deck furniture. Then he realized Sofia wouldn't be able to reach her glass from the lounge chair where he planned to see her settled. He moved everything to the glass table where they had eaten each meal he'd shared with the family and slid the short table to where Sofia could easily reach it, finally returning the glasses to the little table.

By then Sofia appeared. She took in all that he'd done, then wordlessly settled on the lounge chair. He handed her the ice pack. A cool breeze ruffled his hair, and he dashed inside for a blanket. The days were nearly the longest of the year, but the heat of summer wouldn't be here for another couple weeks. Right now, evenings could still cool down, especially since the house blocked the western sun. He returned with the blanket as she set the boot aside and rested the ice pack on her foot.

"You think of everything." She picked up a glass of lemonade, and he laid the blanket across her lap. "Are you sure I'm not keeping you?"

"Not at all." He rested his hand on her shoulder, and she seemed to sink into his touch.

"Thank you, Nathaniel. For everything."

He touched her cheek before he realized he'd done it, then escaped to his own chair. The scent of flowers moved on the breeze. He inhaled, attempting to categorize each bloom. The sweet dogwood. The pungent lilac. The gentle rose.

"What brought about the special relationship you have with the Allens?" Sofia tugged his attention away from thoughts of flowers.

"As a kid I spent most of my Saturdays with them while my parents worked. Still do, I suppose. I mow their lawn, help them with manual labor they claim they're not getting too old for." He rested his elbows on his knees. "I'm not sure how I'm going to keep up with Mrs. Allen's garden. It's going to take off soon, and I'm going to have too much produce on my hands."

"I've never seen a garden as big as hers. What does she grow?" Dodger put his chin on Sofia's chair, looking for a pet. Sofia obliged and rested her head back against the lounge chair, eyes on the dog.

"She grows everything." He made a mental note to help Sofia down to see the garden. "Right now it's primarily blackberries and strawberries. The squash will begin to take off, and the rest of the vegetables will follow. In fact, please help yourself to anything out there."

"Oh, I couldn't—"

"It'd be a favor to me. I'll need to visit a couple times a week to harvest everything, but the boys can help, too." A thought took root. "And I'll leave you some of the produce. Better than me attempting to can it like she does. Or make a pie. I usually come over here after the rest of my clients are taken care of for the day, so no earlier than four." Though all that might change if the Town Circle bid was accepted.

"Of course it's fine, Nathaniel." She shifted the blanket to remove the ice, then settled back in her seat. "You know, Mrs. Allen has continued to provide me with more details about you than I could have asked for." She chuckled. "And that was after her initial information the first day."

Nathaniel felt heat rising in his cheeks. "I hope it was all good."

"Considering she specifically wanted me to know you were single?"

Nathaniel stuffed down the embarrassment at that and laughed. "She didn't even tell me her house sitter was female. After you arrived she provided the same information on you, I'm afraid." And then some.

Her cheeks turned a pretty shade of red, like a pair of Ballerina Red flowers, blooming on her cheeks. In that moment, Nathaniel wished two things. Not because he felt he had to obey God, but because he wanted to of his own free will. He desired to understand all of what Sofia experienced, including the hardships Mrs. Allen had told him about. And find a way to comfort her. That last thought struck a chord in his heart he hadn't felt for years, and it unnerved him.

"Tell me about your family?" Sofia asked, thankfully changing the subject.

Nathaniel nodded. "I'm the middle of three boys. All of us still live here, as do our parents. My dad is a foreman at one of the local dairy farms, and my mom is a legal assistant. Neither seem ready to retire."

"Do your brothers work with you on landscaping?"

"Nope. My little brother is building up his own farm, and my big bro teaches phys ed at the high school. He loves it. Runs sports camps over the summer. Drivers ed, too, I think." Nathaniel scrambled for what he could ask her to keep the conversation going. "Do you like your job?"

"Being an administrative assistant for my church has been a blessing since the boys moved in with me. I can flex my hours to match their school schedule. Though summer has proved difficult." She set her glass on the table.

He waited to see if she'd go on, but when she didn't, he asked, "How'd you hurt your foot?"

Sofia rolled her eyes. "I made a wrong move while hauling something out of storage. Thought I sprained it at first, but the X-ray showed differently. I think because I injured it at work, my pastor wanted to give it plenty of time to heal."

"I sense there's more to it?"

Sofia rubbed her fingers. "It means I won't help put together the Fourth of July parade float. Our church has created one every year for as long as I remember. I'm usually in charge of it. However, the boys are more important, so it's fallen to another church member."

"But it's important to you."

"It is." Sofia swiped at a tear sneaking down her cheek, and Nathaniel's heart twisted. "This is the first year Anna won't be there, and now neither will I."

The ringing of his phone broke into the conversation, making Sofia jump. Nathaniel glanced at the caller ID. "It's the mayor."

Sofia clasped her hands as if she were praying—and maybe she was. Nathaniel walked to the end of the deck, hand shaking as he pressed the green answer button. His future would be dictated by the next few minutes, but he glanced over his shoulder, not fully willing to let their conversation go.

Chapter Four

Sofia watched Nathaniel, one hand pressing his phone to his ear, the other massaging his neck. Stars were beginning to pop out overhead as the sun continued its path toward the western horizon. It would be darker here than in the city, without the street lights to which she was accustomed. It'd been a dark period the last several months, too—as dark as she anticipated tonight's sky would be.

Grief and discouragement had run roughshod over her heart. This evening, she'd genuinely laughed. It felt good and strange. Now she simply felt sleepy. Not bone-tired like usual, and she knew she owed that fact solely to Nathaniel Turner.

Sofia ran her hand over Dodger's short fur. He hadn't left her side since she sat down, but he raised his head now, watching his master take what appeared to be a tense phone call. She hoped that didn't bode ill for him. She appreciated his presence and, though it'd been just a few days, she could see him as a friend. He seemed good for the boys, too, and that was most important.

It meant she wanted this deal to work out for him. With his passionate presentation and personal investment, he was the right person for the job. Would the cranky old ladies of the town have a better candidate? Sofia hadn't stayed for any of the other presentations, nor the question and answer time. The boys were too restless for that, and it wasn't their town. They'd been there for Nathaniel.

He pushed his phone into the pocket of his jeans, a faraway look on his face. She hesitated to break him out of his thoughts, nervous for him and the answer he'd received.

He looked over at her. "I got it. I got the contract."

"Nathaniel! That's wonderful! Congratulations!"

Nathaniel laughed, wonder written across his handsome face. "I'm still marveling over it. All the work I did—with your help—to put together that presentation. The vision I have for it. Sofia, the council voted unanimously for my bid. Unanimously."

Sofia swung her feet to the ground and hopped on one foot, beckoning Nathaniel closer. He came immediately to her side, and she flung her arms around his neck. "I'm so proud of you!"

He tightened his hold on her for just a moment before he eased back. His eyes contained a mix of joy and concern. "It'll be a lot of extra work, especially with the Allens' garden produce to worry about."

"We'll help you with that, like you suggested. The boost this project gives your business will make every night ahead worth it. If people like your work, they'll hire you for their projects."

Nathaniel blew out a breath. "That was a big reason I wanted this project. I'm already stretched to the maximum capacity of clients, so I needed this break if I wanted to hire on more workers."

"There is another reason." And she had an inkling of what it was. She'd pieced together enough of his story over the past several days.

Nathaniel shoved his hands in his pockets.

"You have memories there, too. It's a personal project. I know."

He studied her. Looking for what?

"Truly, Nathaniel, I'm so happy for you."

"I appreciate you being happy for me after everything you've been through. It can't be easy and—"

Sofia held up her hand. "There's a Proverb that says something about good news being like water to a thirsty soul."

Nathaniel stared at her another long moment, and she could see his mind working.

"You're making me antsy, what's up?"

"Sorry. I had an idea and attempted to guess your reaction before I brought it up."

"Sounds ominous."

"I hope not." Nathaniel helped her sit before sliding his chair a couple inches closer. "You've reminded me that I come from a solid home with good parents who love God and brothers who had my back even if they annoyed me. But the Allens gave me purpose. Their love of the outdoors, and their garden in particular, gave me a similar passion. It's why I opened my own landscaping business in the first place. I'd like to offer the same to your nephews."

"We already talked about the boys helping you with harvesting the garden."

"Would you bring them to the Town Circle to work with me there?"

"Nathaniel, I couldn't. They'd distract you from your work."

"My proposal included asking for community volunteers, and hard, muddy work is just the type I think your nephews will relish, considering the way they've been following me around Mrs. A's garden. You can be our overseer, staying off your foot until it heals."

Sofia shook her head.

"Full disclosure?" He patted his pocket where he kept his phone, "Mrs. Allen mentioned the boys getting into trouble."

Sofia dropped her chin.

"I'm not judging, Sofia. And my offer isn't because I think you can't handle the boys. I had plenty of people looking out for me when I was a kid, and I still got into trouble. However, I didn't have the kind of loss your nephews have faced. But I understand it."

"I came here to get the boys away from their friends. I didn't anticipate they'd build relationships we'd have to leave when we return home." Indecision had her folding her arms. How could she know what was best for the boys? She wanted to say no, keep their distance the way she originally planned, but truthfully, she wanted to help Nathaniel, and she knew the boys would enjoy it, too.

"I don't expect you to take Mrs. Allen's word on everything about me. If you're worried—"

"As glowing recommendations go, hers was a supernova." Sofia's heart beat faster, as the idea of helping Nathaniel with his project took root. The earnestness in his expression, the genuine care in his eyes, made her feel anything but alone. And she suspected her nephews would love to spend more time with him.

Sofia let out a slow breath. *God, am I doing the right thing for Rowen and Tucker?* Could Nathaniel be the answer to her prayers? The person who could finally help her get through to her nephews? But what would happen when they left for home? The boys would lose another person they cared about.

Her phone dinged, and she glanced at it. Pastor Flores. Learned Nate Turner is tending the Allens' garden. Went on a retreat with him. Good man. Glad to hear you have someone looking after you in a strange town in the middle of nowhere.

Tears pricked Sofia's eyes for the umpteenth time, but she rarely got such a clear answer to a prayer. Maybe the fallout to a temporary friendship wouldn't be as terrible as she thought. It wasn't as if they'd lose him like they did Anna, since they could still drive up to see Nathaniel after they returned home.

What about your heart?

She couldn't think about herself. Everything she did had to be in the best interest of her nephews, and she'd already made sure Nathaniel understood friendship was all the relationship she could offer, no matter what Mrs. Allen suggested. As long as her own broken heart cooperated, she'd come out of this situation just fine.

Sofia squared her shoulders. "All right, let's do it."

Nathaniel's smile made her heart skip. Yup. She was in trouble already.

Wednesday afternoon, Sofia sat on the deck in the lounge chair, her foot elevated with ice, watching the boys play catch, her book lost in her lap as her thoughts distracted her from her favorite pastime. The sun shone brightly after a day of rain. A day they hadn't seen Nathaniel, and it felt like he'd taken the sunshine with him. Which wasn't true, seeing that it now warmed her shoulders, dried the ground and heated the air.

Ever since their conversation Monday night, she'd been hard-pressed to keep him out of her mind. He'd left with promises to let her know when the boys could help him in the Town Circle. Almost two full days and no word whatsoever. Had Nathaniel changed his mind? Could he think the boys would handle the garden alone?

If he did, it would take away his one reason for visiting, and they wouldn't see him as often. That should be a good thing, except the boys had been asking after him for the past two days, and she didn't know what to tell them. Sure, she could have texted Nathaniel, but that felt presumptuous. Instead, she'd been checking her watch every few minutes. It closed in on five o'clock, so perhaps he wouldn't make it over today, either.

Of course, that would help him manage his busy schedule now that he had a timeline to finish the Town Circle. She just wasn't sure what to make of the disappointment that coursed through her. The feeling came from her nephews' expectations, right? She sought the boys out now. They were on the far side of the garden, throwing sticks into the retention pond.

The idea of Nathaniel being a good role model for them had grown on her in the past forty-eight hours. And she couldn't deny how much his presence helped her stay off her foot, which had been improving since they arrived in River Cove last week. At least until the rain yesterday. That made it ache something fierce. And today she hadn't managed to stay off it very much. The boys had been antsy after being cooped up. None of which had anything to do with Nathaniel, and she'd keep telling herself that until she believed it because the idea of a summer romance—at her age—was all sorts of ridiculous.

She couldn't count the number of teen girls who came back to youth group every fall only to stop in her office for a piece of the dark chocolate she kept on her desk and spill distraught tales of their summer breakups. It broke her heart, and she spent most of September praying for them, until they'd gotten over their heartache and moved on in time for homecoming. They came for chocolate to celebrate then, too, and tell her all about their choice of dress. Yes, the last thing she needed to do was act like a teen girl when she had bigger worries, like her nephews.

Who were getting rather close to the edge of the pond. Had she instructed them to stay away? She couldn't remember if it was one of the rules she'd laid out but made note to make that clear as soon as possible, because if they made a misstep and fell in, there was no way she could reach them quickly enough. Anxiety shot up, and she hopped on her good foot to the edge of the deck.

"Hey, boys!" She shouted and waved.

They turned toward her and waved back.

Before she could yell across the lawn to warn the boys to stay away from the pond, her phone rang. One glance at the caller ID and her emotions swirled. She needed to take this call.

"Boys!" She shouted again and picked up the phone. "Hey, Heidi, what can I do for you?" She pinned her gaze on the boys, willing them away from the pond.

Heidi let out a huge sigh. "I'm so glad I caught you. I know you're on vacation, and Pastor Flores said not to bother you, but it's about the Fourth of July parade float."

Sofia rubbed her chest, as if that could ease the ache there. "Can you start at the beginning? How far have you gotten?" The boys grabbed their ball and backed away from the pond. *Thank you, God.*

"Uh, well. I'm staring at the frame you got out of storage."

That's as far as Heidi had gotten? "Do you have the folder I left? It lays out all the orders, supplies and the plans."

"What plans?" Shuffling came on the line. "You mean the diagrams? Yeah, Pastor Flores gave them to me, but I don't understand them."

Sofia took a deep breath to keep her tone gentle. Heidi hadn't put together a float before, but she was the only person Pastor Flores had been able to get to replace Sofia at such short notice. "They'll walk you through, step-by-step, on how to build the float. It's like building one of those build-it-yourself bookshelves."

"I hate those. Why can't we use the same float as last year?"

Sofia eased into the nearest chair, sticking out her left foot to take the pressure off it, the deck warm on her bare heel. "Because we use a lot of live materials that don't keep from year to year."

"I don't get why we do this float anyway."

Sofia clenched her teeth. Why had Pastor Flores thought Heidi could handle this job? "Because it's a wonderful way to be a part of the community. Now, look at page one. It's the overview. Do you see the scene we want to create? It's the same design as last year, so you'll have a foundation to start with."

"Yeah, the lady liberty. I found the costume. Who is going to play her?"

"You'll have to find a volunteer. I usually ask one of the teen girls."

"Ah. And the bunting. It looks waterlogged and unusable."

"Waterlogged?" Sofia dropped her head to her knees. How could this be happening?

A wet nose nudged Sofia's hair, and she looked up only to get a doggy kiss to the face. "It's good to see you, too, Dodger," she whispered as she patted his sides. He rolled over, showing his underside, and Sofia obliged his request for belly rubs.

"The chicken wire is all here." Heidi seemed to be talking to herself more than Sofia. "And the arches—I remember we tied red, white and blue balloons to that."

A shout brought Sofia's attention to the yard in time to see the boys break into a run toward the house. Dodger wiggled away and raced toward the boys. She couldn't help but smile at the mutual enthusiasm, even as darker emotions churned thanks to Heidi's call.

"Oh, now I see the order you put in for carnations and ivy. And the candy. Okay. I'll see about building the platform and finding a volunteer. Sorry to bother you." Heidi hung up before Sofia could respond.

Sofia dropped the phone onto the table. Her heart hurt, her head spun and her ears rang. The float meant everything to her. It was a red, white and blue floral float—the entry requirements for the parade—with a live Statue of Liberty and the name of the church along the side. Sometimes one of the church musicians would play guitar, too. It was such a fun way to bless the children who lined up along the parade route.

Would Heidi be able to pull it together, or would this be the first year everyone—including Anna—would miss their church float?

A warm hand rested on her back, and she straightened, looking up at the tall man beside her. Wow, it was good to see him. A question flashed across Nathaniel's features before he held out a hand. She grasped it, and he easily assisted her to her feet, then helped her hop over to the lounge chair where she'd left her boot.

"Thanks." She wanted to say so much more to him. She never got tongue-tied and prided herself at being able to maneuver around any situation—a necessary skill as an administrative assistant. Yet, here she appeared like an awkward middle schooler.

Nathaniel knelt in front of her, holding the boot for her to slip her foot into it, as if he held a glass slipper. She wanted to smack her head. Why was she letting him help her?

"Do you have a plan for dinner?"

Okay, not the greeting she expected. Why wasn't he grilling her about the phone call? Or any other of the myriad questions that filled her own head right now. Like why he hadn't visited yesterday and what brought him over today.

She fastened the boot straps in place, the scratching sound pulling her into the present moment. "Mrs. Allen stocked plenty of pizza, and that always goes over well with the boys." In fact, where were those two right now?

"Pizza, huh?" Nathaniel glanced over his shoulder just as she spotted the boys tumbling in the bright green grass with Dodger. How dirty would they all be by bedtime? "What if we get carryout from the pizza place in town and take it to the Town Circle? Tonight's the last night to see the old version before I start refurbishing."

"I see what you're doing." She threw up her defenses, her emotions too turbulent to find solid footing. "You're trying to get my mind off that phone call."

"Is that what I'm doing?" Nathaniel gave a cheeky grin, threatening to take down the wall she'd just put up. "Or am I aiming to make one last memory of the old place?"

Oh! She liked the way she felt when he looked at her like that. It chased all the cold, dark places away and wrapped her in a warm blanket of peace.

Nathaniel handed Sofia her crutches, happy to see the worry lines around her mouth relax into a smile. Not that he should be paying attention to the way her mouth looked. He scrubbed his face. He was supposed to be helping her, not thinking about getting emotionally close to her. Let alone kissing her! He didn't want his heart involved in this and had promised her nothing more than friendship.

"Long day for you?" Sofia situated her crutches under her arms. She wore a cute purple sleeveless top that showed off the ripple of her muscles as she adjusted her position. It was all absolutely adorable.

Turner! Knock it off.

"Lots of paperwork and phone calls to get things moving for the Town Circle project. I put in rush orders for the flowers, stone and rocks, pond pieces and all the other supplies." In signing the final contract, he'd discovered a monetary penalty for not finishing on time. He had too much invested to dispute it. Anyway, he wanted it done by the Fourth for April's sake. "Since I have the design all created and itemized for cost, I already had the quotes ready. I just needed to tell my suppliers to send the orders through and set up delivery. I also confirmed the required permits are set—those went through yesterday—and the equipment I'll need should be delivered tomorrow."

"Productive." And she sounded suitably impressed, which bolstered his confidence that he could actually deliver on the project like he'd promised. It also scared him because he hadn't had any inclination to impress a girl since April had his heart.

He shoved those emotions away. "I thought so. The rainy day yesterday helped. I'm already struggling to keep up with the administrative details." Flashing lights went off in his brain. "You're an administrative assistant."

"Yes, yes I am." Her cheeks bloomed like two round dahlias.

"Administrative details are the biggest hole in my operation right now. I'm hopeful that the financial boost this job will bring in will provide me the opportunity to hire someone to fill that role. Not that I'm trying to interview you for the job." Then again, why would that be such a bad idea? "I'm just acknowledging a weak area of mine. I'm much better at design and landscaping."

"Since I can't do much because of this—" she waved her booted foot "—I could manage the administrative details. Though, I don't know the industry or have the relationships to draw on, which will slow me down."

It wouldn't for long, Nathaniel was sure of that.

"But please tell me how I can help." The way she shrugged said she missed being busy, that sitting around with her foot up irked her. Aiding him wasn't personal, and he'd best keep his focus on that. By giving her a task, he was benefiting her, not giving himself another excuse to interact with her.

Like he'd told her, part of his plan for growing the business was adding an administrative person. Someone who could coordinate the people he hoped to hire to take over the regular lawn care he currently managed—not that he minded mowing like he did admin tasks. Then he could focus on the design part of his business. However, none of that had anything to do with why he liked the idea of Sofia's participation, and his rambling proved it.

He needed to change the subject. Now.

"Let's start by getting those boys fed." He nodded toward the two rascals who were racing up and down the lawn with Dodger.

Dodger had paced the house all day yesterday and today, until they'd pulled up to the Allens' curb. He'd never seen Dodger that excited to get anywhere. Usually he sat contentedly at Nathaniel's side, wherever that may be.

The boys turned toward the irrigation pond, and a thought struck him. "Have the boys been playing back there, by the water?"

Sadie nodded. "They discovered it today. I was a little worried because there was no way I could get to them fast enough if they fell in."

"Can they swim?"

"I think so?" Her face paled. "I actually don't know. I remember my sister taking them for lessons." She pressed fingers to her forehead. "There's so much I don't know. Should know."

He couldn't help it. He wrapped an arm around her shoulder. She tucked under his chin, and he brought his other arm around her. It felt wonderful to hold her.

He shouldn't be doing this, not if he wanted to keep a platonic distance. He rubbed her arm and put space between them. "It's an easy question to figure out and put your mind at ease. Come on, let's go ask them."

She nodded and followed him down the deck steps to the grass. He stayed beside her as she navigated the uneven terrain with her crutches. Each step wobbled, but he held back from offering to help. The set of her jaw said such a suggestion would not be welcome.

But she would tire herself out needlessly. "How about I call them to us?"

Sofia huffed out a breath. "Fine. I hate this, you know? I can hardly fend for myself, let alone keep up after them. Was coming here really a good idea? If my mother-in-law knew, she'd swoop in here and take the boys. I promised Anna I'd care for them. Deathbed promises mean something, you know. And she gave me, not her mother-in-law, custody. She trusted me with her most precious loves."

"Hey." Nathaniel circled around to get in front of her, ducking down to look her right in the eye. "I know something about death-bed promises, and I don't take them lightly. And you aren't in this alone right now. I'm here to help you."

"But you have—"

Nathaniel held up a finger. "I wasn't finished. I'd like to introduce you to my mom."

Red as deep as a Dianthus flower covered her entire face, and he realized his mistake.

"I didn't mean it *that* way. I meant that she works part-time and is used to three rambunctious boys—my brothers and I weren't perfect—so I'm sure she would welcome a little chaos back into her home. I've heard her mention how quiet it is, and, yes, it's usually in the context of grandkids, but she knows better than to pressure me about that these days."

The red didn't diffuse any, but Sofia cocked her head at his last sentence. Heaven help him, his mouth was getting him in too deep.

"Deathbed promises. You understand grief."

Nathaniel inhaled a shaky breath. "I was engaged a few years ago."

"Is she the real reason you wanted the Town Circle bid?"

That brought his chin up. Her brown eyes

were so filled with understanding, he found himself wanting to open up to her.

Sofia smiled. "You talked about the business benefits and yet were personally invested, so I knew there was more to it than fond childhood memories."

"There is." Nathaniel swallowed. "She died."

Sofia adjusted her crutch to free her hand and wrap her fingers around his. "I'm sorry, Nathaniel."

How had he gotten himself here? Where he wanted to talk about April with Sofia. Wanted to tell her about the woman who captured his heart as a teenager. Number one rule of dating was to not talk about past relationships, right? But they weren't dating. They were only friends, and friends shared about heartache. Didn't they?

"Do you think your mom would be interested in pizza?" Sofia asked, obviously giving them an out from the unexpectedly deep topic.

"I shouldn't have—"

She stopped his apology. "It was a good idea. It's kinda lonely here during the days, and I don't have a mom I can talk to. Maybe I can borrow yours while I'm here."

How could he not grant her wish? "I'll give her a call."

Chapter Five

In the passenger seat of Nathaniel's truck, Sofia tapped her thumb on the edge of her crutches, which were tucked in next to her. Not only had Mrs. Turner let them invite themselves over for a pizza dinner, the woman sounded ecstatic about the idea when Nathaniel called her. So excited that Sofia had heard her side of the conversation even though Nathaniel hadn't had his cell on Speaker.

What possessed Sofia to suggest the idea? Other than the mix of good feelings Nathaniel's hug had given her and the sorrow in his eyes when he mentioned his engagement. He knew heartache, and it broke her heart that this kind man had experienced it. What could she say that would help? She hadn't found the words to help her own grief.

Fortunately, Rowen and Tucker asked Nathaniel a hundred questions, particularly about the antics he'd gotten into as a boy, so Sofia had no need to speak. Though Sofia wasn't sure her nephews needed ideas to fuel their escapades. At least she didn't need to worry about whether they could swim. Nathaniel not only discovered that fact but extracted their assurances that they would stay away from the retention pond. She suspected the boys would listen to him better than if Sofia made them promise the same.

They turned off onto a long, paved drive. Nathaniel grew up in a large frame farmhouse set back off a quiet country road just outside town. Trees blocked it from view until Nathaniel pulled into the large front yard. Mrs. Turner had the front door open as he put his truck in Park. Sofia's stomach turned in circles.

"Are you ready?" He glanced at her, and she nodded, because what other answer could she give?

"Whoa, this is your house?" Rowen said from the back seat.

"Dodger, sit!" Tucker whined. "You're hitting me with your tail!"

Nathaniel grinned at Sofia, then got out

and opened the back door. Dodger jumped to the ground and raced up to Mrs. Turner. Rowen and Tucker weren't far behind, though they beelined it for the massive wooden play structure.

By the time Sofia gathered her purse and crutches, Nathaniel waited at her open door with his hand extended. The warm summer breeze ruffled her hair, and she shoved a strand out of her face before passing the crutches to Nathaniel. As self-conscious as it made her feel, she appreciated his help because getting out of the truck with her boot was nearly impossible without someone to balance her.

"The boys are going to sleep well tonight." Nathaniel's hand closed around hers, warm and comforting. His voice created an intimate feeling Sofia needed to push away. They were barely friends, and she wanted to respect his revelation about his lost fiancée. She wasn't here to replace her, even if she was in the market for a relationship, which she wasn't.

"The fresh air has been good for all of us." Sofia made conversation to cover her thoughts. "I haven't heard a sullen word from the boys all week. I worry what it'll mean when I tell them we have to give the Allens their house back." She needed to remind everyone of that fact.

Nathaniel laughed. "I have a sneaking suspicion the Allens would invite you to stay if you gave even a hint of it."

"I couldn't—oh, you're joking."

"Not really." Nathaniel slammed the truck door and winked. "Come on. My mom's self-control is probably holding by a thread. Another minute and she'll be over here helping you to the door herself."

Disoriented by Nathaniel's teasing—it had to be teasing, right?—Sofia was grateful for the warmth of his hand at her back. And when they rounded the hood of his truck, she was even more grateful for his sturdy strength. Mrs. Turner barreled toward them. Had she a tail like Dodger, it would have been wagging. That image nearly made Sofia laugh out loud and effectively calmed her nerves.

The older woman's long silver hair was tied up in a massive messy bun, and she wore round, dark-framed glasses. Her tanned skin stood out from her light-colored peasant shirt. She even wore several hemp necklaces wrapped around her neck. Sofia could picture her more like a wood nymph as a young girl, and she had to wonder whether Nathaniel got his love of plants from his mom.

"Welcome!" Mrs. Turner threw open her arms and wrapped them around Sofia, crutches and all. She smelled of a flower... lilac, lavender, something heady like that. "You must call me Eileen. I'm so glad Nathaniel invited you over. I've missed having boys in this house and you—" she held Sofia at arm's length "—need a rest. Come sit on the porch. Nathaniel, let your father know you're here."

Nathaniel waited a beat to catch Sofia's eye. It wasn't until she gave a slight nod that he said, "Sure thing. He out back?"

"Where else?" Eileen Turner laughed. "He's trying to fix some motor for Simon." To Sofia, she added, "He's my youngest."

As soon as Nathaniel disappeared around the side of the house, Eileen released Sofia and walked beside her. "Tell me which boy is which."

"Is it all right for them to be on the play set?" Tucker pumped his legs, getting his swing to go dangerously high. Rowen climbed the rock wall that led up to the tower, which was even with the second floor of the house.

"Of course it is." Eileen waved away the

t she loved them with everything she
she'd do anything for them. *Lord,*
worry and strengthen my faith in You
You love these boys more than I ever

niel rounded the side of the house,
or his dad. He loved visiting the old
veet childhood memories filled the
the play set, the house. Visiting his
l pops held none of the bitter echoes
s diagnosis, like his apartment did—
tment they were to share together.
home was a nostalgic reprieve from
that chained his heart.

n blinded him as he crossed the back
veen the house and the outbuildings.
ed into the shade, then ducked into
shop. How many times had he found
here, like this?

tcha working on, Pops?" Nathaniel
n the door frame.

mall room was shadowed except for
rescent spotlight shining over the
ch. Various tools were scattered over
, and even more hung from the walls.
ed to tinker, and this was his favor-
e to spend his spare time. The floor

concern. "My boys spent hours and hours on
there. And it's as sturdy now as it was then.
Don't you worry."

"But what if they fall?"

Eileen stopped. "Boys are bound to do
that, you know? Girls, too, I reckon, though I
don't know from experience. Have they tried
climbing any trees yet?"

Sofia shuddered. "At the moment, I'm
trying to decide if city danger is worse than
country danger."

"Danger is danger, sure. Probably easier
to contain it in the city, what with fences
and parks, but the way you said 'city danger' makes me think it wasn't them running
in front of a car that you're worried about."

Sofia started. How had this woman read
her so easily? "No, that wasn't what I was
thinking at all."

"Because if that was the case, it would be
the same danger here as there." Eileen cocked
her head, several strands of gray hair coming loose from her bun. "I can see you have a
specific danger in mind. What is it that worries you?"

Sofia stuttered until she decided she
might as well be honest with this woman.
As a mother of boys who'd grown to adult-

hood, she understood. And considering Nathaniel's gentlemanly ways, she did a right fine job raising them. She was also one of the only people who dug into how Sofia was handling instant motherhood. Most people worried about how the boys were adjusting—and she wouldn't have said well until coming to River Cove. Emotion clogged her throat. Coming here had been the right plan, but what would happen when she had to take them back home?

Eileen ran her hand down Sofia's arm, compassion in her eyes. "How long have you been their caretaker?"

"Since Thanksgiving. It's been tough. I thought I was at least managing, until two weeks ago. I had just fractured my foot when they were caught shoplifting. My little nephews. It's one of the reasons we came here. To get away from the friends who egged them on."

"Mmm-hmm. You know there are stores here where children can shoplift? And friends who are both good influences and bad."

"Are you trying to make the city seem safer?"

"Oh, no, my dear." No smile, not teasing or joking. "I'm showing you that it doesn't

matter the location. Da[...] will always be there fo[...] mothers is to guide a[...] she chuckled.

Mothers. Pray. "But [...]

"I know. But you are [...] and praying for them [...] would."

Sofia blinked away [...] against her eyes. She [...] so very much. But may[...] as much as she ought. [...] the worry?"

Eileen looked over [...] could see through it to [...] gone. "I'm not sure you [...] matter how old your b[...] as a reminder to pray. [...] turn your worry into f[...]

Sofia nodded, the w[...] soul. Tucker squealed [...] top of the fulcrum, han[...] fore swinging the opp[...] reached the tower. Sofi[...] back.

She wanted to sque[...] huge hug, make sure [...] much she loved them. [...]

was spotless, yet it smelled of sawdust, metal and turpentine.

"Ah, you're finally here." Pops grabbed a dirty old rag and wiped his greasy fingers. A small engine lay on the table before him. "The engine on Simon's automatic mucker thingamabob went out, so I'm trying to fix it. It'll keep until after supper. Already put in the order for pizza."

"Thanks, Pops." Nathaniel crossed his arms, an odd feeling of emotion swelling in his chest. He loved his parents. Visited at least once a week. Saw them at church. Yet, somehow, he felt like he took them for granted, and that was the last thing he wanted to do. "I really appreciate you dropping everything to invite us over."

"Aw, nah, it's not trouble at all. What's this all about? You look tense, son." Pops tossed the rag on the table and tugged on the string attached to the overhead light, plunging the room into semidarkness. "Something wrong with you? Or is it about that landscaping bid? I hear rumblings about it in town."

"It's nothin'." Nathaniel shrugged. "Nothing to worry about." Nothing for Pops to worry about, that's for sure.

"Humph. It's something, all right. Maybe

nothin' worrisome, but it ain't nothin'." Pops put his arm over Nathaniel's shoulder, turning him toward the sunlight. "It wouldn't happen to be those two young men you brought with you tonight?"

"No, of course not. Why would they have anything to do with—" Nathaniel pinched the bridge of his nose as they excited the workshop. "There's nothing wrong, Pops." What did he see that made him think something was wrong? He'd brought Sofia here to help cheer her up, not because of anything to do with him. And no way could Pops sense his conflicted feelings over Sofia.

Pops chuckled. "Protesting too much, ain't ya?"

Nathaniel opened his mouth to protest some more, then snapped it shut.

Pops laughed and led him toward the front of the house. "I like seeing you this way, son. All out of sorts and confused. It means something's going on in here." He poked Nathaniel's chest. "And it's often about a woman. So spill."

"Pops." His face heated. "Nothing's going on anywhere." And definitely not with Sofia. Anyway, how had he gotten into this conversation, and how did he get them out of it?

"Uh-huh. You keep telling yourself that.

Way I see it, last girl you brought home was April, and you've never brought kids and their single mother over to meet your parents."

Way to say it like it was. "It's not like that, Pops."

"It ain't? Then you didn't invite a single mom and her boys—excuse me, her nephews—over for pizza?"

Nathaniel groaned. "Of course I did, but—"

"But nothin'. You've gotten close to them in a short amount of time. I gots ears, ya know. I heard when they arrived, and I spotted them at your presentation on Saturday. I ain't sayin' it's bad, mind ya, just that it's something different. Something you ain't done in a long while. And maybe it's somethin' good." Pops's bushy eyebrows lowered. "I know it's been tough these last few years."

"I don't want to talk about that." About April.

"No, we don't have to. I know it's still sore for ya. But I don't think that drawn look on your face has anything to do with her, neither. It's the same look I saw in my own eyes when you were a boy, maybe still do, though my eyesight ain't what it used to be. Anyway, it's part worry, part concern, part caring. Frankly, it's the look of a dad."

"A what?" If Pops socked him with a right hook, Nathaniel wouldn't have been more surprised. He skidded to a halt at the side of the house. "What does *that* have to do with anything?"

Pops laughed. "You care about those boys or you wouldn't have brought them here."

"Sure I do, but a…" *Dad?* Not Nathaniel. Maybe not ever. Because he'd only dreamed of being a dad with April, with the kids they'd have together. When she died, he gave that up. Not to mention that meant he and Sofia would have to be together, and there was no way that could happen. They'd agreed to be friends, and he would keep his promise to her.

"I see that brain of yours working overtime, calculating a way out of this conversation and away from those feelings inside. I know what I see." Pops tapped his own temple. "I s'pose I'll let you off the hook since your young lady and her boys are here. She's mighty pretty, ain't she?"

Flames might as well have been boiling Nathaniel alive. Of all the things for Pops to say!

"Aha! You can't hide that kind of thing from me, son. I've known you all your life, and I can read you like a book."

How had he gone from having nostalgic thoughts about his old man to having Pops needle him about…a future Nathaniel had thought he'd buried right alongside his fiancée?

Nathaniel stuffed his hands into the pockets of his jeans and took off for the front of the house. When Pops didn't follow, he turned around to walk backward. "You coming or not? Mom's gonna have my hide if I don't drag you with me."

Pops laughed. "I wouldn't miss meeting your gal for the world."

Nathaniel flopped his head back. Sofia wasn't his girl.

But for once, the idea wasn't as painful as usual.

Fortunately Sofia was saved from her unexpected conversation with Eileen by the arrival of Nathaniel and his dad. Dodger left the boys to race up to the older man, who squatted to welcome the energetic dog.

Mr. Turner had a weathered face and white hair, with a twinkle in his eye that warned Sofia she may have more teasing from him than anyone else. Or maybe he would direct the teasing at Nathaniel. Considering the red tinge of Nathaniel's cheeks, perhaps he already had.

"It's been entirely too long since Nathaniel has brought a friend to see his old folks. You can call me Paul." He reached well-used hands out for Sofia, clutching her shoulders, a welcoming smile beaming from him like a lighthouse. "I'm giddy to meet you, dear, and cannot wait to greet your nephews."

"They found your swing set." Sofia pointed with her crutch.

"Of course they did!" Paul didn't turn to look at them. His gaze studied Sofia, and she began to squirm.

"Hey, Pops?" Nathaniel tapped his arm.

"Just makin' sure, son." Paul took one more look at Sofia's face, which had to be as red as a tomato. "Yup, I believe I'm right."

"Pops." Nathaniel's warning elicited a smile from his dad. Nathaniel shook his head. "You know, I don't want to know. Not tonight."

Paul chuckled. "You'll figure it out soon enough. I'm right sure of that." He wrapped his wife's hand around his arm. "What do you say we greet those two youngsters? Nathaniel can get Sofia settled on the porch just fine."

"It's a lovely plan, my dear." Eileen gave her son a significant look, then let her husband lead her toward the boys, Dodger on their heels.

O-kaay. There was a ton of loaded *something* in all of that. As soon as the older pair were out of earshot, Sofia leaned toward Nathaniel. "Why do I feel like there was significant subtext happening just now?"

"Because there was." Nathaniel folded his arms, his beard not softening the downturn of his lips. Sofia jerked her gaze away. "It wasn't directed at you, though, so don't worry. And there won't be any pressure from that department."

From what department? What was she missing? Were his parents thinking she and Nathaniel were an item? They weren't, but would it be so bad if they were? She glanced at Nathaniel. He appeared anything but happy, excited or intrigued by the idea.

Which meant that, if Nathaniel had no interest in changing his mind about being single—likely due to his loss—she needed to keep her own mind from even entertaining the concept.

She pushed the idea away and focused on Nathaniel's parents. They were effusive in their greeting of Sofia's nephews. Tucker's bright expression showed he welcomed them in return. Eileen sat on the swing next to him and seemed to be engaging him in conversation. The little boy animatedly responded to everything she said. However, Rowen kept his young face shuttered.

"It's good to see him happy. Tucker, that is." Sofia spoke quietly, unsure whether to include Nathaniel in her contemplation. It's what a friend would do, so it had to be okay, right?

"My mom is good at that. Whenever we had a bad day, she'd come out and sit on the swing with us. In no time, we'd tell her all our problems."

Sofia risked a glance at Nathaniel. He watched his mom and Tucker with such a tender expression, her heart released a tiny *aw*.

The moment snapped closed when Sofia spotted Paul pointing at something up in the tower for Rowen to look at. Rowen disappeared for a minute, then returned, excitement lighting his features. This wasn't time to open her heart to Nathaniel. Rowen and Paul were up to mischief.

"What did Rowen find?" Sofia asked Nathaniel, prepared to dash across the lawn as fast as her crutches could carry her.

"Probably the zip line." He said it so nonchalantly.

"The what!" Why wasn't he running to stop them? She adjusted her crutches to sprint across the lawn. Nathaniel stopped her forward momentum with a hand to her shoulder.

"My dad will attach it to that tree down over there." Nathaniel pointed twenty feet from the tower. "Best way to get down. Fastest, too. And way better than jumping, which was my youngest brother's preference until Dad installed the zip line."

"You're giving me heartburn." Sofia pressed a hand to her chest.

He squeezed her shoulder with a gentle pressure that told her he heard her fear. "I remember my parents saying that us three boys were going to find things to get into, and they'd prefer those activities done within safe parameters. Of course I didn't understand what it meant at the time, but now I see how my parents directed our escapades. Watch how careful my pops is with Rowen, how he triple-checks the line. And we thought we were so daring." Suddenly Nathaniel turned to her. "If you don't want him on the zip line, just tell me. I'll make sure my folks follow your instructions."

Sofia opened her mouth to do just that, until she spotted Rowen zipping down from the tower. He squealed, and when he reached the end, dropped to roll on the ground, laughing. Sweet, wonderful laughter that brought tears to Sofia's eyes and painful relief to her heart.

Then Rowen jumped up and high-fived Mr. Turner. "I'm totally doing that again!"

She hadn't heard him express even a smidge of the joy he'd just portrayed since Anna was killed. A tear splashed down her cheek, and she adjusted her crutch so she could wrap her arm around Nathaniel's. It was something more than a friend would do, but at the moment, she couldn't let herself care. Her emotions were too big, too complex, and she needed his grounding.

He didn't stiffen at her touch, so she rested her head against his shoulder. "Let him have fun." It was time for the boys to laugh again.

Chapter Six

Thursday morning, Nathaniel pulled into the parking area at the entrance to the Town Circle. The day held much promise. The sun rose with the hope of a bright, warm day, but without the humidity of midsummer. Perfect for working outside, and he had a lot to accomplish today if he hoped to get this project finished by the Fourth. He'd uncharacteristically left himself no room for error or weather delays. It meant too much to—

He punched his brakes. Standing below the Welcome to the Town Circle sign, and blocking what amounted to the park entrance, stood a gathering of about twenty-five people, all holding signs protesting the Circle refurbishing. He recognized each person, most of them older women from the church. A few of the older men who usually hung out in the diner. And a couple of moms with their children in strollers.

Then he spotted Mrs. Reynolds. She stood on a short stool, bullhorn in hand, shouting encouragement to the protesters who'd gathered.

Nathaniel strategically parked off to the side so he could carry his tools past them. Interacting with protestors was not part of his plan for the day. Dodger stuck his head between the seats. Nathaniel rarely left Dodger at home unless he met a new client. Dogs were allowed on the Circle, but now he was rethinking letting Dodger join him. And not just his dog.

Dodger's tail thumped against the back seat. Nathaniel adjusted his sunglasses and straightened his ball cap. Stalling. That's what he was doing. It wouldn't phase Nathaniel to wade through this opposition to get his job done, and Dodger would stay by his side if he told him to. Except that Sofia and the boys would be here in an hour, and he didn't want them mixed up in whatever this was. Picturing them attempting to push through the crowd, calm as it was, made his gut churn. Maybe he'd text Sofia not to come today.

Unless he could get the crowd to disperse. He wouldn't let them stop him from doing his city-appointed, contract job. He respected Mrs. Reynolds's opinion, but in this case, he didn't understand why she held the stance she did. Over 95 percent of their town of one thousand voted for the renovations. And why wouldn't they want their most iconic community space to look more beautiful and function better?

Nathaniel braced himself for what he might have to face getting past the line of protesters. Then again, what physical harm could Mrs. Reynolds do? Nathaniel outweighed her by double.

He'd barely slammed the door of his truck when a wet, slimy something smacked into his face, halting his tracks. He ran his fingers through the goo, and some landed on his lips. Blackberry? A pie tin dropped at his feet. Someone wasted a good blackberry pie by throwing it at his head? Now, *that* should be a crime.

Dodger barked from inside the truck, and Nathaniel crossed his arms, scowling. Mrs. Reynolds looked triumphant from her spot under the arch. Nathaniel took a deep breath. He needed to keep this situation calm, not escalate it.

"If you wanted to give me a pie, Mrs. Reynolds," he called to her, "next time, try to keep it level so I can eat it."

Her jaw dropped, and the crowd murmured bits of laughter. Nathaniel left much of the mess all over his face, wiping just his eyes clean so he could see, shouldered his shovels and released Dodger from the car. Without another word, he pushed through the picketers until Mrs. Reynolds stopped him four feet into the Circle. Dodger paced uneasily by Nathaniel's legs, so Nathaniel gave the dog a command to sit.

Mrs. Reynolds glared at Dodger before turning her anger on Nathaniel. "You have to leave the Circle alone. I didn't want you to get this job. You've had enough emotional pain. You don't need more. Why are you leaving me no choice?"

What in the word did that mean? "I'm sorry, Mrs. Reynolds. The people voted to revitalize our Town Circle, and I have to do my job, so you need to let me through."

She raised her bullhorn and aimed it right in his face. "I won't."

Nathaniel sighed, but her distraction with the bullhorn allowed him to edge past her. Dodger stayed right at his side.

"I won't stop, Nathaniel Turner." Mrs. Reynold's voice followed him. "You should be ashamed of yourself, ripping up the sod and destroying a place we hold in our hearts."

He wasn't destroying it. Although it would look like it for the first week. He planned to resod in order to level out the ground—save a few turned ankles—dig a hole for the pond and lay gravel for the stone walkways.

He'd already made arrangements to donate the current sod to the elementary school and replace the metal picnic benches with wooden ones his father made. It was his way of saving what was held dear while making it look like new. And if Mrs. Reynolds had been paying attention at the presentation, she'd know that.

"April would be appalled." The bullhorn shouted her words at his back as he aimed for the place he planned to build the stone-tiered flower bed, with a bench for taking the perfect outdoor pictures. "She's probably rolling over in her grave that you would be the one to disgrace—"

"Stop!" His word was a pebble to her bullhorn. Her words hurt in ways he couldn't express.

"It's true and you know it. She loved this space."

He knew, all right. April adored the Town Circle, and that's exactly why Nathaniel wanted this contract.

"You know she took her first steps here? Her mother told me. She also told me April lost a tooth here when she was in third grade. And you would tear up her memory. Just like that."

The verbal blow felt like a physical one. It dropped Nathaniel to his knees, and he wanted to cover his ears like a child as Mrs. Reynolds's taunts kept coming. Dodger shoved his nose in Nathaniel's face.

"Why would you disgrace her memory? Or have you replaced her already?" The bullhorn trumpeted through the green space.

Nathaniel froze. Mrs. Reynolds already knew about Sofia. Knew his connection to her. If he responded, she'd know how much he wanted to protect Sofia, and she'd know exactly how she could get to him.

Yes, hearing about April hurt like someone had sent a javelin through his heart. But standing by as his job inflicted pain on someone else, someone who was hurting as much as he was, well, that was an entirely different story. One he would not allow to happen.

That meant figuring out why Mrs. Reynolds was so against refurbishing the Town Circle, and why she'd made it personal. If he could answer those two questions, perhaps he had a chance of keeping the older woman away from Sofia and getting this job done before the Fourth of July.

Because Mrs. Reynolds had one thing right: April deserved to have her favorite place ready in time for the holiday. Her memory warranted nothing less.

Sofia parked the car beside Nathaniel's truck, surprised—and more than a little concerned—to see the gathering of protesters. "Boys, you stay close to me."

Should she even let the boys out of the car? Was it safe? Should she call Nathaniel first? They were a little early. The boys had been too excited to help Nathaniel today so she'd agreed to leave the house before time.

"Why are all those people here?" Tucker asked over the click of his seat belt releasing.

"They're angry." Rowen observed. "And that's the lady from the other day."

He was right. Mrs. Reynolds, the lady who'd confronted Nathaniel at the town hall, stood with a bullhorn, shouting toward the center of the Circle. Around her, several people were chanting with their fists pounding the air. Then Sofia realized most of the protesters appeared around Mrs. Reynolds's age. Why would the older population of River Cove be against this project?

"I'm going to find Nathaniel." Tucker threw open his door.

"Tucker, wait!"

But Tucker dashed out his door, Rowen racing after him. They disappeared into the crowd before Sofia could gather her crutches. Helplessness sparked her anger. The boys might be enjoying the vacation, but they still needed to listen to her. She balanced on her crutches and slammed the car door.

"Look! It's the woman he's dating!" someone in the crowd shouted, pointing at her.

Sofia backed against her car, the sun shining down like a spotlight. Sweat trickled down her temple. "I'm not dating anyone."

But the crowd didn't hear her, or if they did, they didn't care.

Mrs. Reynolds aimed the bullhorn at Sofia. "Why would you encourage one of our own sons to tear down a local treasure? You're an outsider who has turned his head. He wouldn't be doing this if it wasn't for you!"

Was that true? She'd brought her nephews

to River Cove to escape trouble, not cause it, and she'd never want to hurt Nathaniel. Mrs. Reynolds's words buzzed around Sofia's head like angry hornets as the crowd pressed closer. And where were her boys? She needed to find them. Now! She couldn't lose them.

Fear strengthened her limbs, and she used her crutches to force herself through the crowd, stepping on toes if people didn't get out of her way.

"Let me through. Please let me through." She needed to see her nephews. Make sure the boys were okay, safe. Nathaniel, too, but he could take care of himself. The boys were her responsibility, and she'd brought them to this mess. She had to get them out of it.

"Sofia!" Nathaniel appeared at her side and helped her push through the last of the crowd. "I already called reinforcements. Are you okay?"

"The boys. Where are my boys?" Sofia's heart pounded, her breath huffing in short gasps. She scanned the green space for them. There. Her boys were safe and unharmed on the far side of the Circle, far away from the crowd, Dodger keeping them safe. Her knees buckled, and Nathaniel's arm wrapped around her waist, keeping her upright.

"They're fine. Eager to start working with me." Nathaniel's voice was in her ear...close, comforting.

The crowd. "Nathaniel, wait." She tried to pull away, but Nathaniel didn't budge.

"I don't care what they see." Steel hardened his tone. "I won't let you walk this alone."

She stared at him, his face so close to hers. His eyes were stormy, his jaw tight. Somewhere in the distance she thought she heard a siren. "I'm sorry, Nathaniel."

His features relaxed. "There's nothing for you to be sorry about, Sofia. You hear me? Nothing."

Sofia nodded, unable to reply. How could all the oxygen have disappeared when they were out in the fresh, clean country air? But her lungs couldn't find any. Not here in Nathaniel's arms, his voice comforting and his words touching the wounded places in her soul.

Nathaniel's cheek twitched under his trimmed beard. They'd stopped moving there in the middle of the green where everyone could see and stare, and—worse—she didn't want to break the spell! Then she realized the far side of his face was stained purple. She touched whatever it was to find it sticky. She yanked her hand away.

"Blackberry pie." Nathaniel's nose scrunched, and he wiped his cheek. "I usually prefer to eat it than wear it."

"Please clear the area," a disembodied voice boomed.

Sofia yanked her attention away from Nathaniel. Two police cars had arrived in the parking area, and one policeman spoke with Mrs. Reynolds while the other held a bullhorn and directed the crowd.

Nathaniel released Sofia, leaving her unsteady. Why did she wish to stay in his embrace? It didn't make sense.

Nathaniel adjusted her crutches under her arms as she struggled to bring her mind back to the present moment. He winked, and her face flamed hot. Did he know what she was thinking?

Her nephews and Dodger came running, Tucker jabbering about the activity by the parking lot. Nathaniel stayed close while letting her navigate the rough grass herself as they made their way to the dispersing crowd. As much as she wanted him to keep his arm around her, it wasn't practical with her crutches. They were very unromantic.

Ugh! Why was she thinking of romance again? She needed to focus on her nephews. Needed to disprove what Mrs. Reynolds claimed about her dating Nathaniel. Was she dating Nathaniel? She couldn't. Anything that took her attention away from her nephews was off-limits.

"Why are those people mad?" Rowen's question yanked Nathaniel from the cauldron churning in his head.

"I need to find out." Nathaniel stopped his little group, like a dad would stop his family, aiming to protect a wife and kids. Boy did he need to get his head on right.

He looked over to the entrance where the crowd was dissipating under the guidance of a policewoman. It would be safer for Sofia to take the boys back to the Allens' house, away from the tumult this project sparked. Sending them home was the last thing he wanted to do. If he were completely honest, he wanted to act on the emotion he'd felt while holding Sofia in his arms. He wanted to hold her again. He wanted to kiss her.

He shoved his hands through his hair, his fingers sticking where they ran into blackberry filling. "Sofia, are you sure you want to stay to help? I can walk you to your car. The boys can help me in a different way."

She sighed. "The boys have been too excited about this morning for me to take them home without a mutiny." She glanced at the side of his face that took the brunt of the pie. She'd pulled away when she touched it—could she find it repulsive?

"Turner, you all okay?" The female officer shouted across the open space. She shaded her eyes with her hand.

Nope. No, he wasn't okay. He waved. "Be right there!" He considered her, and when she offered him a soft smile and nodded for him to go on alone, he relaxed. Whatever her reasons, she didn't find him so repulsive or the situation so dangerous she wanted to flee.

By the time he jogged up to Officer Rain Keller, the mayor's baby sister, the entire entrance was empty of people and cars, save for Nathaniel's truck, Sofia's sedan and Rain's squad car.

"Not what I anticipated when I submitted my bid." Nathaniel took the towel she offered him.

"I don't doubt it." Rain rested her hands on her utility belt. Petite in stature, she made up for it in spunk. "Richard hasn't told me much—I suppose he can't as mayor—but Mrs. Reynolds has it in for this project."

"Do you know why?" He wiped the blackberry filling from his face.

"She never gave me a reason for her actions. The rest of the crowd either didn't want the interruption, hates the mess and mud or are cantankerous enough to despise change."

Nathaniel coughed out a humorless laugh. "I can guess who those last people are."

Rain grinned. It gave her face a youthful glow. It also made Nathaniel want to look out for her like he would a little sister, if he had one.

"You know I'll be fine here, right?" He knew that was not what he should be saying at all. If Sofia and her nephews planned to keep helping him, he wanted a police presence the entire time.

Rain's smile turned to a scowl. "You're not saying that because I'm a girl, are you?"

Nathaniel rubbed the towel over the back of his neck.

Rain huffed. "When am I going to be taken seriously if all people see is that I'm young, a girl and the mayor's sister?"

Nathaniel gave a sheepish shrug. "Never?"

"Then answer me this." She jabbed a finger into his shoulder. "Are you dating that woman like Mrs. Reynolds says?"

Nathaniel looked over his shoulder, watching as Sofia herded her nephews back toward where he'd left his tools. Dodger stayed close to them, too. His heart swelled.

"I'll take that as a yes."

Nathaniel snapped back around. "It's a no, Rain. Sofia and I are not dating."

"Save it. I've watched my big brothers claim the same thing too many times not to recognize it plain as day. You can count on me to keep an eye on the park, especially when your girl and her nephews help you out." She held up the finger she'd used to jab him. "On one condition. You see me as a cop. Deal?"

"Yes, ma'am." He saluted.

"Oh, give me that towel and get back to work. We need this place shipshape before the holiday."

Sofia relaxed when Nathaniel finally made his way toward them. For safety reasons, not because she saw the easy way he interacted with the female police officer. The boys and Dodger ran to greet him.

"Guess the excitement's over and it's time to get to work." Nathaniel adjusted his ball cap, then took his sunglasses from where they'd been sitting on the brim of his hat and put them over his eyes. "Boys, you ready to get muddy?"

The boys whooped and Sofia laughed. Tension seeped out of her body.

After he washed his face with a jug of water he retrieved from his truck, Nathaniel set up a chair for her and then showed the boys how to measure out the spaces he was creating. He used spray paint to mark areas, then pounded in wooden spikes and strung twine between them. Yes, she watched him a mite too closely than she ought, but her emotions were all out of whack, and she couldn't make them behave.

"Are you sure I can't help?" Sofia asked Nathaniel when he returned what was left of the twine to his supply pile. "There has to be something I can do."

Nathaniel rubbed his lower lip then fished out a notebook. "I have an idea. Here's a list of suppliers you can call. With the July Fourth deadline fast approaching, I want to make sure to stay in front of any delays."

The deadline also reminded her of Heidi's call, and she was tempted to check in with her substitute. Sorely tempted. But she knew she needed to leave the float in Heidi's hands. The purpose of this trip was to get away, even from coordinating the float. Pastor Flores thought Heidi capable, and if she needed help, she'd call again. Sofia had to trust her...with sweet memories Sofia worried would be gone with her sister.

When lunchtime rolled around, Nathaniel and the boys were stacking squares of sod taken from where the pond would go. Cell phone and notebook resting in her lap, she took a moment to simply watch them. Dirt smudged their calves, arms and faces. The boys' laughter danced across the lawn. Nathaniel's deep voice rumbled. His muscles flexed as he carried another square to his wheelbarrow.

Sofia scratched the sweat that had dried at her temple. The scene looked entirely too... familial. As if she and Nathaniel were married and the boys were their own biological sons. It caused an ache to develop in her chest. She'd never worried too much about whether she'd marry or have kids. She loved being an aunt. Now...

Eileen Turner's words came back to her, words about being a mother. She also recalled the visceral fear when the boys had disappeared into the protesters this morning. Was that what it meant to be a mother? Was she becoming that for her nephews?

And what of Nathaniel's place in their lives? The boys obviously looked up to him already. But this was temporary. She had a job to get back to, and the boys had school to return to.

Sofia glanced down at the notebook, filled with her notes from the phone calls made on Nathaniel's behalf. She'd been working for him, doing the same things she did for Pastor Flores, just Nathaniel was a landscaper, not a pastor.

Or was he a pastor of sorts? Cultivating a garden, only this one was the hearts of two orphaned boys. She needed to be mindful of those tender little hearts. They had already been broken, losing first their father then their mother. She couldn't cause them more pain by participating in a summer romance that would leave them all worse off than when they'd arrived. Perhaps putting some distance between the boys and Nathaniel would be wise, too.

Another round of laughter, shared by all three—boys and man—reached her. It might already be too late to remind the boys they wouldn't see Nathaniel again after this summer, but it wasn't too late for her. She'd make sure the boys knew Nathaniel would be a friend they would remember fondly from the summer they spent healing in River Cove.

Nothing more.

Chapter Seven

As dusk darkened the sky Friday night, Nathaniel dropped into the driver's seat of his truck. Covered in mud and aching in places he thought he'd already built muscle, he didn't have the energy to even start his truck, let alone drive home. Dodger, muddy and looking as weary as Nathaniel felt, whined from the back seat.

What would it be like if we had more than an empty apartment waiting for us?

The question blasted him like the AC vent that blew cold air at his face. He once dreamed what it would be like to return home to a family after a long day's work. Maybe cut out early to catch a child's ball game. Whisk his wife away for a date. But that wasn't his lot. Instead he would work until the sun went down to recreate this green space for other families to enjoy. Not his own. Not anymore.

What about Sofia and Rowen and Tucker?

Nathaniel jammed his truck into Reverse. Wasn't his brain as tired as his body? It should be too tired to chatter. He blew out a breath, then made sure to take extra care to look around before backing out of the space. There was no cause to be careless in a place where children frequented.

He turned left onto Main Street, then a right, and another left onto the street where his apartment sat above a shoe repair shop. His work timeline meant closing the Town Circle for two weeks while the sod set. Making sure it would reopen before the Fourth of July meant closing it no later than Monday. He could have closed it today but decided to risk the small buffer in order to allow families to have one last weekend to enjoy it.

This afternoon, he'd dug the hole for the pond. The bobcat he'd rented got him started, but most of the hole he'd dug by hand, especially to get the shape right. Tomorrow he'd meet the electrician to lay in the pond mold and set up the pump. Monday he'd cut the sod. Tuesday he'd lay the new rolls. While that took root, he'd build the picture arbor, pond area and entrance archway. Two weeks and a couple days is all the time he had left. If he didn't make it, he wouldn't be paid the full amount, making business expansion impossible and disappointing April's memory.

It's Friday.

Friday? What his brain meant by reminding him of a random day of the week, he didn't know. Fridays were nothing special anymore. While most people celebrated the end of the workweek—and his brothers often tried to get him to join them for a movie or something—he always worked on Saturdays. Ever since April died, Friday nights—

He slapped the steering wheel, causing Dodger to bark at him from the back seat. Now he knew what he'd meant to remember: Rowen and Tucker told him about their Friday ice cream nights. He needed to show up for one while they were here. Why hadn't he put it in his phone to remind him?

Or trust God to bring it to mind, like perhaps He had?

He let that thought simmer while he braked at the last stop sign on Second Street. If he trusted that God was finally speaking to him again, he wasn't sure he wanted to hear what He had to say. After all, God let April die.

Still, Nathaniel knew he should keep talking to God. Yet all Nathaniel did was tell God how much his heart hurt, how much he missed April. It felt like he lived in the dull, cold, brown days of March and God said nothing.

But are you ready for the vibrancy of summer?

The thought hit him like a shovel to the back of the head. He wasn't ready for anything. He knew he was still mired in a past he had no interest in forgetting. Forgetting meant leaving April, and the happy future they'd dreamed of together, behind.

An image of Sofia's smiling face crossed his mind.

If—and it was a big *if*—she was attracted to him, was interested in a relationship and saw potential in being together, none of that mattered. Sofia and her nephews were leaving when the summer ended. He knew that and couldn't let helping her sidetrack him from reality. He'd promised himself he wouldn't let his heart get involved.

He nearly squealed his tires pulling onto his street. Dodger grumbled, but Nathaniel couldn't get out of the truck cab—or his head—fast enough. Being this physically tired shouldn't allow his mind to work over-time. He didn't want to deal with it.

Giving Dodger a bath momentarily dis-tracted him, until his own shower gave his mind time to think again. He turned those thoughts into a prayer. Not really a prayer, a one-sided conversation, reminding God that he had been willing to obey Him, to help Sofia and the boys—because it was *God* who asked him to do so. He didn't sign up to get his heart involved.

By the time he dressed in basketball shorts and an old T-shirt, he collapsed on his sofa exhausted and a little miffed at God. Prayer definitely had not improved his mood. Work-ing on the ground April loved so much was supposed to be an act of memorial to her. Yet he couldn't get Sofia off his mind.

Dodger rested his chin on Nathaniel's knee and Nathaniel rubbed the dog's head. "What do you think, boy?" *I'm so confused.* He wished he had a person he could talk to in-stead of a dog. Dodger was a great listener and all, but he needed someone to tell him what to do.

He already knew what Pops would say. *Son, you gotta give it all to God.* Humph. Or his brothers: *Get out of the house and stop working all the time.* He had no interest in catching a movie or attending a ball game, not when he used to do those things with April. What else was there to do other than work?

Sofia would know.

She would know what to say, too. Maybe that's why he was so mixed up. She understood loss. Perhaps what he dealt with was the need to work through his grief over April rather than any feelings for Sofia. If he looked at her as a friend—nothing more—then he could talk to Sofia about April. Sofia would understand.

The sun had nearly set, however, and it closed in on nine o'clock. Too late to visit. Right? It wouldn't hurt to drive by and see if the lights were on at the Allens' house, would it?

"Come on, Dodge." Nathaniel reached for his cell, and Dodger's tail wagged. Nathaniel tapped the phone on the arm of his sofa, doubt surfacing. "It's late, but I could go check the garden, see how the boys have been handling the harvest. I'll need a light, but I haven't harvested anything for a couple days, and Mrs. A would be disappointed if I let any of those blackberries go to waste."

Dodger cocked his head. Even his dog

could see through such a flimsy excuse. Harvesting blackberries in the dark. Nathaniel massaged his head.

Blackberries. The memory of getting assaulted with a pie roared back. More like what came after. His pounding heart as he raced to protect Sofia. Then holding her in his arms. The thought of kissing her. In April's favorite place.

"Dodger, come on. We gotta get out of here."

Dodger pranced around Nathaniel's legs as he grabbed his wallet, keys and left his usual baseball cap home. He swung by the grocery, picked up three different flavors of ice cream then drove out to the Allens'.

It was a risk, showing up unannounced after eight thirty at night, ice cream in hand, but Nathaniel couldn't bring himself to text Sofia ahead of time. He didn't want to give her a chance to refuse him. Of course, if she wasn't up for company or asked him to leave, he would. But he would have seen her first, and he was too tired to explore exactly why that mattered.

Lights were on inside the house—a positive sign. Should he go to the front door or circle around back as if checking the garden was his only motive for being here?

Dodger stuck his head between the seats, tongue hanging out, as if to ask what Nathaniel was waiting for.

"Good question." Nathaniel scratched the dog's ear, gathering his courage. "Let's go."

Dodger's tail wagged, and he emitted a quick bark. Nathaniel had barely gotten the rear door open when Dodger took off for the backyard. Guess that made his decision. Hopefully Dodger's entrance would smooth the way for his arrival.

Nathaniel grabbed the bag of ice cream and followed Dodger around the house.

Sofia wanted to break something. Or maybe just send the boys to bed so she could sit down. Finally. Her ankle throbbed and her head ached.

So much for no more sullen words. All day the boys nagged her about going to the Town Circle to help Nathaniel, but she'd said no. She didn't want to bother him or cause trouble with the protesters. Not to mention, she needed to slow down the growing relationship they had with Nathaniel since they would leave at the end of the summer. But did Rowen and Tucker understand? No. Nope. And definitely not.

concern. "My boys spent hours and hours on there. And it's as sturdy now as it was then. Don't you worry."

"But what if they fall?"

Eileen stopped. "Boys are bound to do that, you know? Girls, too, I reckon, though I don't know from experience. Have they tried climbing any trees yet?"

Sofia shuddered. "At the moment, I'm trying to decide if city danger is worse than country danger."

"Danger is danger, sure. Probably easier to contain it in the city, what with fences and parks, but the way you said 'city danger' makes me think it wasn't them running in front of a car that you're worried about."

Sofia started. How had this woman read her so easily? "No, that wasn't what I was thinking at all."

"Because if that was the case, it would be the same danger here as there." Eileen cocked her head, several strands of gray hair coming loose from her bun. "I can see you have a specific danger in mind. What is it that worries you?"

Sofia stuttered until she decided she might as well be honest with this woman. As a mother of boys who'd grown to adulthood, she understood. And considering Nathaniel's gentlemanly ways, she did a right fine job raising them. She was also one of the only people who dug into how Sofia was handling instant motherhood. Most people worried about how the boys were adjusting—and she wouldn't have said well until coming to River Cove. Emotion clogged her throat. Coming here had been the right plan, but what would happen when she had to take them back home?

Eileen ran her hand down Sofia's arm, compassion in her eyes. "How long have you been their caretaker?"

"Since Thanksgiving. It's been tough. I thought I was at least managing, until two weeks ago. I had just fractured my foot when they were caught shoplifting. My little nephews. It's one of the reasons we came here. To get away from the friends who egged them on."

"Mmm-hmm. You know there are stores here where children can shoplift? And friends who are both good influences and bad."

"Are you trying to make the city seem safer?"

"Oh, no, my dear." No smile, not teasing or joking. "I'm showing you that it doesn't matter the location. Dangers and temptations will always be there for our sons. Our job as mothers is to guide and pray. A lot." Now she chuckled.

Mothers. Pray. "But I'm not their mom."

"I know. But you are the one loving them and praying for them just like a mother would."

Sofia blinked away the tears that pressed against her eyes. She did love her nephews, so very much. But maybe she wasn't praying as much as she ought. "How do you combat the worry?"

Eileen looked over at the house, as if she could see through it to where Nathaniel had gone. "I'm not sure you ever will defeat it, no matter how old your boys get. Instead, use it as a reminder to pray. In that way, you can turn your worry into faith."

Sofia nodded, the words sinking into her soul. Tucker squealed as his swing met the top of the fulcrum, hanging for a moment before swinging the opposite way. Rowen had reached the tower. Sofia waved and he waved back.

She wanted to squeeze her nephews in a huge hug, make sure they knew just how much she loved them. No, she'd never replace

Anna, but she loved them with everything she had, and she'd do anything for them. *Lord, take my worry and strengthen my faith in You because You love these boys more than I ever could.*

Nathaniel rounded the side of the house, looking for his dad. He loved visiting the old place. Sweet childhood memories filled the acreage, the play set, the house. Visiting his mom and pops held none of the bitter echoes of April's diagnosis, like his apartment did—the apartment they were to share together. Coming home was a nostalgic reprieve from the pain that chained his heart.

The sun blinded him as he crossed the back area between the house and the outbuildings. He jogged into the shade, then ducked into the workshop. How many times had he found his dad here, like this?

"Whatcha working on, Pops?" Nathaniel leaned on the door frame.

The small room was shadowed except for the fluorescent spotlight shining over the workbench. Various tools were scattered over the table, and even more hung from the walls. Pops liked to tinker, and this was his favorite place to spend his spare time. The floor

Her patience unraveled before lunch, and she apologized for raising her voice three times that afternoon alone. Dinner had been a disaster, and she didn't even bring up their usual ice cream night. Even with the sun casting only a remnant of light from the other side of the house, mentioning the frozen treat might not even get the boys to come inside.

The boys had been out by the pond since dinner. Not in the pond but dangerously close, no matter how many times Sofia nagged them to stay back or reminded them of their promise to Nathaniel. She couldn't go stalking out there with the injury hampering her.

Grrr. If only she could stamp her booted foot without it shooting pain up her leg. The helplessness of her situation caused tears to burn her eyes. Now with the light almost gone, except for the bright deck lights, darkness covered the area past the garden. She could barely see them, and worry increased her agitation.

She'd brought the boys to River Cove to get them away from their natural surroundings, but it hadn't fixed things. Not between her and them. Sure, they'd been well-behaved when Nathaniel was around, but now? When she was alone and denied them what they wanted?

Sofia pressed her hands against the smooth railing of the deck. She balanced on one foot, her crutches forgotten inside. Her calf itched from the boot, and the swelling squeezed her foot. Ice and elevation…that's all she asked for.

Yet, she dare not consider what she wanted. Her first priority was to make sure the boys were okay. She couldn't let herself forget that they were now her priority—she was not a single woman anymore. Her two boys counted on her. Which was another reason she refused to take the boys to the Town Circle today. Nathaniel was good for them, but the connection she'd felt with Nathaniel had to end. She couldn't divide her attention between a man and her nephews. At least not until she figured out this parenting thing, which she was miserably failing at.

Barking brought her attention back to the ever-darkening yard. Dodger raced along the edge of the garden toward the boys. Their shadowed forms jumped away from the pond to welcome him. Laughter floated in the evening air, and a knife stabbed her heart. What a horrible person she was to keep her nephews from Dodger. He made them happy, and they needed happiness in their lives.

We're leaving in a few weeks, and Nathaniel steals my attention away from the boys.

Nevertheless, she couldn't stop her own joy from bubbling up when Nathaniel appeared around the corner of the house. He was dressed the most casual she'd seen him—which showed his ability to dress professionally while working in the dirt. His damp hair was mussed, and he didn't wear his usual ball cap.

He waved and she chewed her lip as he approached, taking the deck steps in two strides to stand beside her. All her good intentions stood as firm a barrier as a cloud of fog.

"Hey." He smiled, tentative and too adorable for her good.

"Hi." Was she really acting like one of the teen girls from church?

"I may be too late, but I brought ice cream." He raised two plastic bags. "Rowen and Tucker may have let it slip that you have a special way to celebrate Friday nights and—" He snapped his mouth shut.

His sweet discomfort washed away her resolve to keep him at arm's length. "We haven't had our ice cream treat yet." Because the boys hadn't been listening. But she couldn't deny them Nathaniel's kindness.

Rowen and Tucker ran toward the house, Dodger on their heels. With a wink, Nathaniel set the ice cream on the table. Then he brought out bowls and spoons from the kitchen and had everything set up before she could do more than maneuver herself out of the way of her rambunctious nephews.

The boys chattered the whole time, and Nathaniel stayed engaged with their conversation. Sofia sat, her foot propped up on a spare chair with ice easing the aching, also thanks to Nathaniel. What was she going to do? Nathaniel was perfect with the boys, and they came out of their grief-encrusted shell when they were with him. She couldn't consider how well he treated her or how her heart felt about it. This was about the boys. It had to be.

But for Rowen and Tucker, she'd do anything. Even risk her heart to spend more time with Nathaniel Turner.

Once again, Nathaniel cleaned up the kitchen while Sofia got the boys to bed. A smile pushed up the corner of his mouth as he thought about those two. They tested their aunt, but they'd lost much of the sullenness he remembered from the first time they met. They reminded him of himself at their age.

Needing space to explore yet boundaries to contain him.

Most surprising, however, was how they seemed to look up to him. It humbled him and made him consider how else he could help them. They were here in River Cove because they'd been having trouble managing their loss. Nathaniel understood that. Perhaps he needed to find a way to take each one aside to see how they were doing. If Sofia approved, of course.

Sofia. The artificial deck light showed the dark circles under her eyes, contrasting them sharply against pale skin. In a word, she looked haggard. Her black hair was a curly mass on her head. Her shoulders sagged. And he couldn't help but notice how swollen her foot looked when he'd given her the ice. She was using it too much.

He tossed the drying towel over his shoulder as he put away the last bowl. Sofia's awkward descent on the stairs warned of her approach. It was late—nearing ten o'clock—and he should go, but he didn't want to. Sure, he'd come over to talk about April and the circles his brain had been running. However, after seeing Sofia, how could he talk about himself? She hadn't joined in much of the conversation over ice cream, and he wanted to understand why.

"You didn't need to clean up." Sofia entered the kitchen on her crutches. "I'm doing more without these sticks getting in the way. Until my foot gets tired, that is."

Nathaniel frowned. No wonder her foot swelled. "Are you ready to be off crutches yet?"

"Dr. Bradley will tell me on Monday. My original doctor told me that after two weeks, I should be able to walk in the boot, as long as I listened to the pain. If it hurts, I gotta get off of it."

"And have you been doing that?" Nathaniel suspected the answer. A bright blush, the color of a hibiscus flower, rose in Sofia's cheeks. "I imagine your nephews don't make it easy."

Sofia shook her head. "Today was tough."

"Then let's rest your foot." Nathaniel hung the towel. "Can I get you something?"

Sofia used her teeth to tug at her lip. "Don't you need to get home?"

"I can stay." *Unless you want me to leave.*

Sofia blinked, then nodded. "Mrs. Allen froze a few batches of her lemonade, and I defrosted one today. It's in the fridge."

"She thinks of everything, doesn't she?"

In no time, they were settled on the back deck, Dodger under their feet. The night air was cool and the sky cloudless. A crackle of tension arched between him and Sofia. Even at this late hour, he reminded himself that his purpose was to help, and Sofia seemed like she needed company.

"How are the boys liking River Cove?" He forced himself to relax in order to make Sofia comfortable, except his leg wouldn't stop bouncing.

"They love it." Sofia had an odd lilt to her statement. "This has been good for them."

"And you?" The question hung in the air, but he didn't regret asking it.

"I… I don't know what to do." Sofia spoke so quietly, he had to lean closer to catch her whole sentence.

"What do you mean?"

She turned troubled eyes on him. "The boys are different here. No, they're different with you."

Nathaniel jerked back, stunned.

"They talk with you. Laugh. And play with Dodger. But when it's just the three of us, they refuse to listen." Her tears glistened in the soft glow of the lantern Mrs. A kept on the table, which Nathaniel had turned on instead of the bright deck lights. "What am I supposed to do, Nathaniel?"

"It's still early in the summer yet." He took her hand. "They're stretching their wings, seeing what life is like outside their grief."

"And I remind them of who they lost." She gripped his fingers. "I miss her, Nathaniel. I miss my sister."

"Aw, I know." He pulled her to her feet and right into his arms. She tucked in close, silent sobs shaking her frame. A tear snuck down his own cheek. He could feel her pain. It was what drew him to her the first minutes they met. He understood it, related to it, battled it himself.

"I'm sorry." She hopped back, swiping at her cheeks. "You're probably tired of seeing me cry."

"Not at all. I only wish you didn't have cause for tears."

"That is the sweetest thing anyone has said to me." She sank into her chair. "You understand."

"I do." The phrase returned to him like a boomerang. He'd said those words to April. Now she was gone. "April and I planned to have a big family. She wanted half a dozen kids and would have loved your nephews."

"Did she live in River Cove?"

"We were high school sweethearts. Once I got my landscaping business making enough of a profit, I asked her to marry me. She wanted a grand, outdoor wedding. Arbor trellis for us to stand under. Flowers in her hair."

"When did she...?"

"We thought her fatigue and weight loss was the stress of wedding planning. I tried to take on more of the tasks, but it turned out she had a fast-metastasizing cancer. Instead of dress fittings, she went to chemo. It didn't even slow it down." Nathaniel swallowed. "Six weeks. That's all I got with her."

"You married her."

"None of our families know. She thought she'd make it to the ceremony. Her mom poured everything into planning our wedding and April refused to take that away from her, but marrying April early gave me access to her in the hospital and her doctors, so we asked the chaplain to perform a small service."

"If no one knows, then she wasn't buried as your wife."

Nathaniel nodded. He'd been tempted to

speak up afterward but couldn't add more hurt to the grief her parents were already facing. April's tombstone made no mention of her true relationship with him. That secret was his alone. And now Sofia carried it with him.

She squeezed his forearm.

"Working on the Town Circle is for her. She loved that space and often daydreamed about having family picnics there once we had half a dozen kids. Mrs. Reynolds threw April in my face yesterday." The pain of it throbbed in his chest. He couldn't fail April again.

"Before I came here, my pastor shared a couple Bible verses with me. He thought they'd help, so I've been reading them each morning. They haven't made a difference to me yet, but perhaps they would encourage you."

Nathaniel nodded for her to go on.

She tapped her phone and read, "Revelation chapter twenty-one, verses four and five. 'And God shall wipe away all tears from their eyes; and there shall be no more death, neither sorrow, nor crying, neither shall there be any more pain: for the former things are passed away... Behold, I make all things new.'"

Emotion clogged Nathaniel's throat. Just as he'd considered before, God wanted to turn the brown grasses of March into the vibrancy of a summer garden. "Thank you, Sofia. I did need to be reminded of that."

"Then, I think it's time for more ice cream." Sofia pushed to her feet, keeping her hand on Nathaniel's arm, not allowing him to stand. Dodger raised his head to watch her. "Don't move. I'll be right back."

Nathaniel rested his elbows on his knees, praying. He'd been right about Sofia's ability to understand his struggle. However, instead of listening to Sofia like she needed tonight, he'd allowed his emotion to keep the focus of their conversation on his problems, not hers. Disappointment at himself overcame the peace the verses had brought. This was why he stayed away from people. Selfishness prevailed, and he only let them down.

Chapter Eight

Monday afternoon, Sofia left Rowen and Tucker with Eileen Turner. The older woman commandeered Mrs. Allen's kitchen to make blackberry pie. The blackberries had ripened so fast and furiously over the weekend, and Eileen had conspired with Sofia to keep Nathaniel away from the Allens' garden so he could concentrate on the Town Circle without worrying about it.

Rain threatened overhead, and Sofia prayed it wouldn't throw off Nathaniel's schedule. Friday night, after she'd brought out more ice cream, they'd shifted to lighter topics. He'd told her of his landscaping plan, which left little room for error. He admitted it was ambitious, but now she understood his motivation. Would Mrs. Reynolds be so against the project if she knew Nathaniel's heart behind his work?

A question for another time. Right now, she opened the door into Dr. Bradley's office, a small clinic a block off Main Street. A receptionist invited her to take a seat while she filled out paperwork. She'd barely finished when the older doctor himself beckoned her down the hall.

"It is good to see you again, Sofia. How are those nephews of yours? I'm sure both of them have been as energetic as ever."

"Indeed." Giving them the blackberry project, and phrasing it as a favor to Nathaniel, had curbed their interest in the pond. For now.

"And your foot? How is it doing?"

"I'm forgetting to use the crutches more and more." Though she used them now.

Dr. Bradley waved her into an exam room. "That's a good sign. How is the pain?"

"By the end of the day, not so good."

"I'm sure you speak mildly." He smiled, dozens of wrinkles creasing beside his eyes. "It is undoubtedly worse than you want me to believe. Have a seat on the exam table."

Sofia wasn't sure what to do with that statement. To have the truth called out in such a matter-of-fact way left her speechless. She set the crutches aside as she maneuvered onto the raised table.

Dr. Bradley took a rolling stool and chuckled. "You are a strong woman who has two rambunctious boys depending on her. I have no doubt you are not resting your foot as much as any doctor would like. Therefore, your foot hurts more than *not so good.*" He held her booted foot in sun-spotted hands and met her gaze. "You must be honest with me, Sofia. Is the pain sharp or dull?"

Okay, then. "It's sharp, especially right on top of my foot."

He released the Velcro and gently pulled her foot free. "Achy all day or only after much use?"

"All day." In fact, it throbbed slightly now that it was free of the boot.

He pressed fingers around her ankle before moving down toward her toes. "How often do you have the sharp pain?"

Sofia felt the heat rising in her cheeks, the embarrassment cut short when he pressed a sore spot and she winced.

Dr. Bradley didn't seem to notice. "It probably hurts a lot by the time you get the boys into their beds for the night, huh?"

"It does."

Dr. Bradley gently let her leg hang and pushed his stool back a few inches. "If you do not rest your foot, it will not heal quickly or properly. I know you are new to town, but I can recommend people whom you can trust to help you with the boys. The Turners, for example."

"Mrs. Turner is watching the boys right now."

"Good, good." He rolled himself over to the desk. "And Nathaniel is helping you with the garden and yard work?"

Were her cheeks on fire? "He does, because the Allens—"

"No need to explain, Sofia. My wife and I would also like to help." He handed her a card. "Give us a call, and we'll have the boys over for a pizza dinner so you can have a quiet evening to yourself."

She stared at the card. "Why would you do that?" Why would a doctor offer to help outside his office? She'd seen him at the Turners' church, but that didn't explain why he'd help a stranger and her nephews.

"You're a single mother now, Sofia." He patted her knee. "My wife and I have a special place in our hearts for single moms."

Sofia nodded, but her mind kept repeating the same phrase: *you're a single mother now*. This wasn't the way it was supposed to be. How could she parent her nephews alone, with no husband or sisterly support? How could she replace Anna as their mother? She squeezed her eyes closed, unable to escape the stark truth. God had placed the boys in her life, just as she was, and that made her a single mom.

Nathaniel parked along the Allens' curb on Wednesday evening, anticipation tightening his chest. Sofia texted him that afternoon to ask him to come by once he'd finished work. He had no idea why she wanted him to visit but made sure to finish up earlier than usual.

His brother Philip had taken over mowing lawns for Nathaniel's business, including the Allens', so Nathaniel could focus on the Town Circle over the next two weeks. The new sod was down—thankfully the rain had stayed light—and his dad had helped him build the Welcome to the Town Circle trellis today. Tomorrow he'd lay the stone walkway. Then finish the pond. Tasks lay heavy on his shoulders, and he prayed for another gentle rain to water the sod.

Though Sofia had brought the boys to work

with him over the last several days, which delighted him, he hadn't had any chance to talk with her since he'd bared his soul Friday night. He was anxious to hear how she'd fared and brought her flowers to say thank-you for relieving him of Mrs. Allen's garden until after July Fourth. The roses' scent wafted a warm smell as he grabbed them from his passenger seat. Maybe he shouldn't have bought them, since it made this feel like a date.

Dodger trotted ahead of him around the back of the house instead of racing ahead like usual. When Nathaniel rounded the corner, the yard was quiet. Trepidation mixed with anticipation. He hadn't misread her text, had he?

"Nathaniel?" Sofia leaned over the deck railing, her round face a cheery bright spot in his day. She looked like she'd slept better the past few days, too. "Come on up. What did you bring there?"

He raised the flowers. "For you. I wanted to say thank you." He hurried to the deck, Dodger following him. "Where are your nephews?"

"At the Bradleys'. Dr. Bradley insisted on giving me a night off. It's been delightful."

Then why had she texted him to stop by? "I won't intrude."

"Nonsense." Sofia waved him to a seat, and he realized she was unencumbered by crutches, though she still wore the boot. A black anchor to her one leg. The other was bare up to the hem of her shorts.

Nathaniel blinked. He didn't need to be noticing that. "How's the foot?"

"Very good today." She leaned a hip against the table. "The rest is helping immensely."

"Then get comfortable. You shouldn't get up as long as I'm here." Heat flared in his cheeks. "I'll get anything you need."

Sofia cocked her head. "You like to serve, don't you?"

Nathaniel shifted uncomfortably. "I haven't thought about it."

"Well, I have something to show you." She waved for him to follow her down the deck steps. "After this, I promise I'll let you wait on me hand and foot."

Without her nephews here, Sofia seemed a different person. Confident. Comfortable. It intrigued him to see this side of her. "Okay, you have me curious."

Sofia grinned and reached for him. "If

you don't mind, may I use your arm? I'm not steady on this grass with the boot."

"Of course!" Nathaniel held out his elbow. He liked the feel of her hand tucked there. Liked it way too much for just being friends. "Are the boys listening any better this week?"

"Somewhat. This task has kept them busy and out of trouble." She wobbled.

"Are you sure you're up for this?"

"Honestly?" They reached Mrs. Allen's tomatoes, and she bent to scratch behind Dodger's ear. Nathaniel waited for her to look back at him. "I haven't walked out here yet. I waited until you got here."

Familiar guilt doused him. "Sofia, if this is too much for you, we can stay on the deck. You don't have to go out of your way for me."

Her mouth turned down. He'd said the wrong thing.

"Never mind." Nathaniel adjusted his ball cap with his free hand. "It's just you seemed happy in your text and then excited when I arrived, but now... Sofia, I don't want you to injure yourself for me. Please." He couldn't bear it if she were hurt because of him.

Sofia stared at him, and his heart pounded. Why did things have to be so complicated? Did she think he pushed for more than friendship? Did he want there to be more between them?

Ugh! This was another reason why he didn't get involved with people. He knew April. April was familiar. April was gone.

A broken tomato stem lay partially on the ground. He bent to snap it off completely, jerking it more than necessary.

"Nathaniel?" Sofia's voice sounded strangled.

He straightened too fast. A wave of dizziness had him stepping into her. She stepped back with a cry. He shook his head clear and wrapped his arm under hers and around her back, supporting her weight as it gave out.

"I'm so sorry." He scanned her from head to boot, fighting the swirling mix of emotion that churned his stomach. "Are you okay? Did I hurt you? That is all my fault."

"I just wanted to show you the blackberries," she whispered.

Her brown eyes were like the richest topsoil. He could get lost in them. His gaze dipped to her lips, which were partly open as if inviting him in for a kiss. Fortunately Dodger whimpered, bringing Nathaniel to his senses.

"Blackberries." Nathaniel repeated what

he'd heard her say. Since she hadn't pulled away or wiggled from his hold, he gently wrapped his free arm under her legs and lifted her to his chest. "What about them?"

She gave a breathy laugh but didn't fight him. He grinned and carried her toward the blackberry patch. There were no ripe blackberries where there should've been dozens.

"What...?" he stammered.

"That's the surprise." Her breath caressed his cheek. "The boys picked all of them for you, and your mom helped them turn the berries into pies. One is inside waiting for us."

He was speechless. Sofia orchestrated this for him?

"Are you...happy?"

He turned his head to find her face inches away. Was he happy? Happy? He couldn't be happy. He tore his eyes away and made for the house. He needed space. Needed to clear his head.

If the heat on his cheek was any indication, Sofia's gaze didn't leave his face as he carried her back to the deck and lowered her into a lounge chair. Then he raised the patio umbrella and positioned it to shade her. Dodger plopped down on the deck beside her.

"I'll be right back." He disappeared into

the house. His heart pounded, and he couldn't make sense of what had just transpired. The last time he felt anything close to what he'd just felt, he was a gangly teenager dancing with April at prom.

He shook the memory away, and his eyes landed on the blackberry pie. Made from blackberries he'd promised Mrs. Allen he'd keep an eye on. Instead, the Town Circle job had stolen his focus. The garden, the lawn, the lawns of all his clients, all sacrificed for the Town Circle.

His temple throbbed, but he returned outside with a dog bowl of water for Dodger and two lemonades. He set the one for Sofia on an end table beside her before he settled in a chair and stretched out his legs. She reclined with an arm over her eyes. Booted foot stretched out, the other leg tucked under it, giving her a vulnerable look. Her burgundy shirt, with a flower-covered square across the top and flared sleeves, made her look small. The mass of hair she had at the back of her head now drooped to the side, spilling in an unruly array of curls.

Dodger pushed his cold nose through Nathaniel's hands, forcing Nathaniel to pet him. He closed his eyes, let his dog comfort him.

It's why he'd gotten Dodger in the first place. They both needed rescuing, needed each other. He'd known it from the first time he met Dodger at the humane society fundraiser.

"I'm okay, boy." Nathaniel rubbed Dodger's head, only to get a lick on the cheek. The dog believed the lie as much as Nathaniel did. A cool breeze offset the hot sun. Or was the heat from under his own skin? Sofia only wanted to show him the blackberries. Innocuous. Friendly. And here he'd turned it into some complicated mess.

"Nathaniel?" Sofia's voice lacked the vibrancy from when he'd arrived, and it captured his attention all the more for its weakness. He'd definitely made a mess of things. She studied him from her lounge chair, the glass of lemonade in her hand. "Is everything all right?"

"Of course. How are you? How's your foot? Are you okay? I'm so sorry I nearly stepped on you." *Shut up, Turner!*

"I asked you first." She waved her hand as if brushing away all his questions. "Are you not feeling well? You seemed dizzy. Are you working too hard? Not drinking enough water?"

He had to chuckle at her mothering.

"I'm fine, Sofia, honest. I just stood up too quickly." Stupid of him. "Please tell me I didn't hurt you."

"Then please stop worrying. It'll be fine."

"That's not an answer to my question."

Sofia looked away, and Nathaniel knew he'd caused her pain. "What can I do?"

She raised an eyebrow. "Go look at what the boys made on the kitchen counter. Then dish us both a piece." She closed her eyes and leaned back against the recliner with a smile—so sweet and gentle that it turned Nathaniel's world upside down.

Sofia rested her head against the back of the lounge chair, marveling at how Nathaniel managed to make her feel safe and comfortable even when her foot felt like it was on fire. She didn't want him to know he'd forced her to put all their combined weight on it. He felt horrible enough.

"Blackberry pie." Nathaniel returned with two plates, each topped with a scoop of vanilla ice cream. He scanned her face, and she found a smile for him.

"Much better than wearing it?" She hoped teasing would ease the tension lines around his eyes and mouth. Instead, they ate in awkward silence for a few minutes. "Tell me about your landscaping. Obviously it's more than mowing lawns. Do you do special projects like the Town Circle often?"

He moved a chunk of ice cream around his plate, turning it purple with blackberry filling. "I enjoy the design side of it. I've designed patios and entrances, poolside views and mailbox gardens. Today I worked on the Town Circle's entrance. A simple arch trellis that will hold a purple clematis vine on each side."

"That will be gorgeous." She could picture it.

"None of the flowers will be in final form when I'm finished, but over the next few years it should fill in nicely. At least, that's my hope."

"Don't discredit yourself." Sofia nudged his shin with her shoe. "You take an idea and turn it into reality. Plus you do it with flowers, which change and grow. You have to have vision to create each unique landscaping design."

A red tinge highlighted his cheeks. "Seeing it finally take form is the best part."

"I understand. I feel that way about the projects I oversee for my church. Seeing an event come to fruition is a joy all its own."

He set his empty plate on the table. "You like your job?"

"I do. Very much. That's what makes all of this so difficult."

Nathaniel frowned. "All of what?"

She hadn't meant to reveal the struggle she'd been battling this week.

Nathaniel took her plate and set it next to his own. "You can tell me."

Sofia lifted her eyes to the wisps of clouds overhead. They were painted on the blue, canvas sky and tinged with the slightest of pinks from the western sun. A warm breeze blew tonight, promising the summer ahead. She had no need to make a decision now, not with weeks to go before they needed to return home. But she would need those weeks to make preparations if she moved ahead with the idea that had begun with her visit to Dr. Bradley.

She looked at Nathaniel. "Remember I told you how every decision I make must have my nephews' best interest at heart? They've been like new boys since we arrived in River Cove. I could see the change within the first day or two, but the disparity between the way they were before we arrived and now has only grown. It's thanks to you. I knew that from the beginning."

"No thanks necessary, Sofia, but you're keeping me in suspense." Nathaniel rested his elbows on his knees. "I'm having trouble guessing where you're going here. You don't need to tell me your whole thought process or defend your ideas to me. It's okay to just blurt out the decision you think you have to make. I want to hear it, and you'll receive no judgment from me. I promise."

Sofia stared at him, weighing his words. He'd opened up to her about his secret; she could share this with him. "In the short time we've been in River Cove, I've had more support in caring for the boys than back home. There has been more understanding, more help. The boys have been better behaved. For their sake, do you think I should consider moving the boys to River Cove?"

Realizing she cared more about his answer than she should, she launched herself out of the lounge chair and escaped into the house as fast as her aching foot could carry her. Embarrassment chasing her all the way.

What if he thought she wanted to move here because of him? Of course, his help was a large part of her reasoning, but she wasn't inviting a romantic relationship. This was all about the boys and what was best for them.

But what if he didn't want her in town? His friendship mattered to her, and she wasn't ready to face his possible rejection. Even if it would protect both their hearts from growing closer than was wise.

Nathaniel folded his hands to create a platform on which to rest his chin. He knew Sofia needed space or he'd have helped her into the house. Instead he sat there, waiting for her and absorbing her words.

Do you think I should consider moving the boys to River Cove?

Did she truly have such little support back home that she'd consider moving to a new community? She'd be leaving her job, her house, her church. Even though her boss sent her to River Cove in the first place—for the boys—Nathaniel doubted the man meant for it to become a permanent situation.

However, he agreed with her that the boys were blossoming here in River Cove. Maybe they would benefit from staying longer, attending school here, joining the church community. They certainly weren't the same surly boys he'd met that first day, at least not around him.

But would the change be good for Sofia?

This asked a lot of her, but she'd do anything for her nephews. It would require a new job, a place to live… What was she thinking? First she unexpectedly takes in the boys, now she's considering uprooting her life for them? Of course she was. She loved them and would do anything for them. Eileen Turner was right, Sofia had become their mom.

He rubbed his fingers over his mouth. Still, he worried for her, and that revelation struck deeply. The attraction he'd felt while holding her in his arms was one thing. The concern he felt right now went much deeper than the desire to kiss her.

Nathaniel raised his eyes to the Allens' garden, forcing his heart not to change rhythms as he remembered the feel of her close to his chest. She was thinking of moving here for the boys, not because of him. He must remember that before his heart ran away with unhelpful feelings.

However, if she moved here, he'd help her find a house, he'd hire her, he'd smooth her way. His parents would, too, and the Bradleys, the Allens… Now he understood why she felt supported here.

He glanced over his shoulder, looking for a sign of her. She was prepared to sacrifice for her nephews, and he was too willing to do whatever he could for her. And that was bad. So very, very bad.

How had he let himself get emotionally entangled with Sofia and her nephews? He'd promised himself he wouldn't, but he couldn't deny how much he cared about her. Them. He would willingly create a position just for Sofia if that's what it took to see her happy when she gave up everything for her nephews.

But where would that leave them—her and him? Their friendship would be confused, that's what. There were already sparks of attraction arching between them. At least on his side, and that unnerved him enough. Them moving here? And Nathaniel helping make it happen? That would just make things worse.

He lowered his forehead to his clasped hands. If only his heart had healed enough to offer more than friendship.

Pain grabbed his chest as the memory of April's final days flashed before him. She hadn't wanted to get married because it would be like saying the cancer won, but she saw the convenience of it, especially that Nathaniel could stay by her side through everything. In the end, however, she left him, and Nathaniel's heart was wrecked, broken into pieces he never expected to ever be put back together.

At Dodger's nudging his hand, he raised glassy eyes to the green yard beyond the deck. Spring was turning to summer, and fruitful life was increasing in abundance. It was the first summer where he saw the disparity between his own life and the gardens he tended. Yet, even in the barrenness of his soul, God was using him to help two orphaned boys and their aunt.

And he had no idea what to do with that.

Sofia hid in the den, too cowardly to discover Nathaniel's answer to her idea. She could see him from where she sat on the sofa, his head bowed. The man had enough to worry about without her adding to his trouble.

She gathered her crutches, her foot too sore to go without them, while she mustered up courage to march—okay, hobble—out there and take back her question before he had to find a way to untangle her from his life.

Nathaniel already felt bad enough that he'd stepped on her foot, but he wasn't to blame for losing his balance and falling into her. It was an accident, even if it probably did set her foot's healing back. And here she'd been hoping she would be free of the crutches, for the most part. Why did healing take so much time?

Her conscience poked at her with that thought. Physical healing wasn't the only thing that took time. Grief and loss took time to heal, too. While she and her nephews had only traveled months on that journey, Nathaniel had for years now, and she knew that's why the boys—and she—connected so well with him. But Nathaniel was not their savior, nor should he be expected to be a part of the boys' healing. Sofia was the parent now, and God...well, He was the Savior, and she needed to put her trust in Him.

Easier said, though, than done.

Mrs. Turner's words about praying to replace the worrying came back to her. She felt like she prayed all the time, but she worried so much, too. She wished she could sit in Pastor Flores's office and talk to him about how to trust God with their futures. He'd know. Maybe Mrs. Turner would, as well. She could ask her.

In the meantime, she needed to let Nathaniel off the hook.

She watched him out the patio window. Sorrow rounded his shoulders like a heavy cloak. He was still healing, just like her nephews were. Like she was. He'd lost a fiancée—no wife—so it was no wonder that emotion would be so deep. Her nephews lost their mother, and while Sofia had lost her, too, she was an adult when it happened, not a child forced to then live with their aunt.

Of all the relationships, Sofia felt like her loss—the loss of her only sister and dearest friend—should be the least, and that she should have recovered already. An untruth, she knew, but as great as her heartache, she couldn't imagine what Nathaniel felt. And here she'd laid an uncomfortable question on him, forcing him to say whether he'd welcome their long-term presence in his community or not. How could she have been so thoughtless?

She pushed open the screen door, and Nathaniel rose to his feet. He frowned as his eyes went to the crutches but waited for her to ask for help, which she didn't. She wouldn't, even if the crutches made everything trickier to manage, like closing the patio door.

She maneuvered until she stood in front of him. He let her set their distance, his hands resting at his sides. When she looked up at him, he swallowed, his scruff rising and falling with his throat, but he remained quiet. His eyes fastened on her.

Sofia took a deep breath. "I'm sorry, Nathaniel. I shouldn't have asked that of you. It put you in an uncomfortable position."

"Stop." He touched her shoulder as gently as she imagined he tended a seedling. He rubbed his thumb against her collarbone, and Sofia had to fight to keep her focus on what she needed to say.

"You're not their parent. That's my responsibility, and I didn't mean to push our need for support onto you." What would it be like to share that burden with him?

"Who is looking after you?" Nathaniel asked, holding her gaze

Had he moved closer?

"You, Sofia." He raised his fingers to her cheek. "Who is taking care of you?"

Tears burned, and her words deserted her completely.

"I told you from the beginning that I want to help. If my presence is helping the boys, I'm glad. Please don't change that on account of me. That's what friends do."

"Do friends do this?" She pressed her hand against his, her crutch slipping away.

"No." Nathaniel framed her face, his eyes

continuing to search hers. "Can we not be friends for one minute?"

"I—"

He stopped her with a kiss. She let her second crutch fall and held his shoulders as he drew her close.

Suddenly, he yanked his lips away. "I'm sorry. I—"

"Don't go around kissing your friends?" She missed his closeness. The strength she felt when he held her.

Nathaniel squeezed his eyes shut.

Sofia wrapped her arms around his waist and rested her ear against his chest so she could hear his pounding heart. It took him a moment, then he held her again, and she never wanted to leave this bubble.

"I can't be more than your friend, Sofia." Nathaniel's voice rumbled around her. "I shouldn't have kissed you. I'm not ready…"

Sofia leaned back just enough to see him. The pain in his eyes broke her heart. "Neither of us are ready for anything but friendship." Which is why she shouldn't have brought up that she was considering moving the boys to River Cove.

He nodded, but it seemed like he wanted to say more.

Sofia's phone chimed at the same time as Nathaniel's.

"It might be the boys." She left Nathaniel's arms to fetch the phone she'd left on the lounge chair and tapped the screen. She met Nathaniel's eyes, the implication of the text caught between them. "Cindy had her twins."

Chapter Nine

Nathaniel carried another twenty-pound stone to the pond area. Each one seemed heavier than the last. He carefully fitted it on the second row. This edging would keep children from accidentally walking into the pond while also being a pretty way to set it apart from the rest of the Circle.

Sweat dripped down his forehead and his back. Officially summer now, the temperature and humidity had risen since last week, promising a summer storm. If he wanted to get the pond finished so he could start crafting the photo arbor area on Monday, he needed to work faster than those clouds blowing in. The sod would love rain, but it would make the stones too slippery to handle. Nathaniel glanced up at the sky. It would be close.

He carried another stone from his truck bed, which he'd backed up as close to the walkway through the sod as he could get. It was slow, lonely going. Normally he would relish this part of his job, a chance to burn through his sorrow with no one for whom he had to remain upbeat. But after another Friday ice cream with Sofia and her nephews last night, he missed them. They were going over to his folks for a barbecue this afternoon. He wanted to be there, but he needed to finish this first.

With the current stone laid, he went back for the next one. He set the stone, the sense of accomplishment energizing him. Until he spotted Mrs. Reynolds parking her car next to his truck. His shoulders sagged at the confrontation he knew to expect. She'd kept a steady stream of protesters, but thankfully they weren't as disruptive as the first day. This morning, only a handful had been at the front entrance, and Mrs. Reynolds hadn't been one of them. What brought her now?

Nathaniel dusted his work gloves on his shorts and strode to meet her.

"Nathaniel, working on a Saturday." The older woman shook her head.

"I made a promise to have everything ready

by the Fourth." He crossed his arms, fighting back the defensiveness that rose in him.

Mrs. Reynolds patted her perfectly curled hair. "I spoke with Richard—Mayor Keller—this morning to express my displeasure over this project going forward."

"What's done is done, Mrs. Reynolds." Couldn't she see how much nicer the sod looked already?

"I realize that." She dug in her purse. "Which is why I've requested a stay of construction order. After you are audited, you may be allowed to resume."

What? "Audited! What for?"

She glared at him through one eye, like an eagle spotting its prey. "I warned you to stay out of this project. I dislike a son of our town getting caught in the middle, but it can't be helped."

"Don't you want this project finished by the holiday?"

"I don't want this project finished at all. It must be stopped." She pulled a peppermint out of her purse. "It's too late to stop you from tearing up the grass, but I can make sure you don't build these monstrosities on our beloved Circle."

"Mrs. Reynolds, I don't understand what

you have against me making our Town Circle better and nicer." Nathaniel yanked his filthy ball cap from his head, slapping it against his thigh. "Why are you doing this?"

"Because it was fine just the way it is. Nothing needs to be *better* or *nicer*." She wagged a finger at him. "It's that type of thinking that's made this all muddled. I hate that the grass has changed. How could you remove the very grass April walked on?"

Nathaniel braced for her words as Mrs. Reynolds barreled forward with her speech.

"Do you realize the memories you have stolen? Memories with our children, our spouses, our loved ones. Memories we can never get back, especially now that you've done…this!" She flung her arms wide, the candy flying and her purse dropping to the crook of her elbow. "But you don't care about April. That much is obvious."

Nathaniel lowered his chin to keep Mrs. Reynolds from seeing any emotion he let escape. He clenched his jaw, willing the tears that pricked his eyes to stay put. This place was filled with bittersweet memories for him, too.

"You know what?" Mrs. Reynolds spat the question. "You probably wouldn't have even gone through with the wedding, for how much care you've shown her."

He swallowed back a sob. If only she knew the truth. If only the town knew how much this project meant to him as April's widower.

"And dating someone else. For shame, Nathaniel Turner. For. Shame."

Was caring for Sofia and her nephews dishonoring April? This project was supposed to be in April's memory. A way for him to give back to her, not make everything worse.

"This is an order for you to stop work at once." She waved a paper under his nose. When had she gotten so close? "The city will contact you regarding the audit."

Nathaniel took the paper—Mrs. Reynolds allowed him to do nothing else—and watched her hike back to her car. His breath came in spastic waves as he waited for her to leave. Then he dropped the paper onto the driver's seat of his truck and went back to hauling stones. If they wanted him to stop, they'd have to send a police officer. For now, he'd work until the rain or darkness made him stop.

He'd skip his folks' barbecue tonight. He was in no mood for company, and, as much as his heart longed for Sofia's company, he needed to put distance between them, too. At least until he figured out whether Mrs. Reynolds was right about him dishonoring April's memory.

Sofia sat on the Turners' front porch, watching her nephews play on the swing set with a few other kids their age. Her foot rested on a cushioned stool, iced tea in her hand. Smoke from the grill floated across the lawn. Various friends of the Turners mingled around, their older and younger sons, too. But there was no sign of Nathaniel. Sofia checked her phone to see if he'd texted or called. Nothing.

Perhaps he'd worked late? He'd told her last night his plan for the next week and a half. She wondered how he'd get everything finished in time, but the way he'd laid it out seemed to say he could. As long as nothing disrupted his plans, like the clouds darkening overhead.

She smiled as Eileen carried over a tray of strawberries, likely from Mrs. Allen's garden.

"How's your foot doing?" Eileen held out the tray. She wore a sleeveless maxi dress covered with earth-tone paisleys.

Sofia chose a perfectly red strawberry.

"Better every day." She bit into the fruit, and summer burst on her tongue.

Eileen sat in the rocking chair beside her. "Have the Allens told you when they'll be returning?"

The strawberry turned flavorless. "Now that Cindy's had her babies and they're doing so well, they estimate they'll only need to spend a week or two in the NICU before being able to go home. Mrs. Allen wants to stay until Cindy is settled, so perhaps a week after that." Three weeks at most before she had to pack up the boys and return to their real life.

"And your job is waiting for you?"

Sofia nodded, her mind going to the Fourth of July float. She'd been tempted to check in with Heidi but had so far contained her desire. She'd even kept herself from asking Pastor Flores about it. Though her boss checked in with her multiple times by text and once by phone, he always focused the conversation on how she and her nephews were doing. Nothing about her duties at the church. She tucked the rest of her strawberry into her napkin.

Eileen set her chair to rocking. "You've been here for so short a time, yet I feel like you've been here forever. You fit in this town,

Sofia. If you would ever consider moving here, we would be happy to have you."

Sofia stared at her. She'd barely voiced that thought to Nathaniel, no one else.

"I know we could rustle up an apartment and job for you. Matter of fact, this old house is feeling mighty empty these days. If the Allens return before you're ready to go back, consider staying here. You'd be welcome for as long as you felt comfortable."

"Did Nathaniel say something?" He wouldn't have.

"About what? Cindy? No, her mom informed the church, and we all received a prayer update." She held out the tray again. "Strawberry?"

"No, about staying in River Cove."

A spark lit in Eileen's eyes as she retracted the tray. "So you have been considering it."

"No. I mean yes. But—" Sofia collapsed back in her chair. "Tell me Nathaniel didn't say anything."

"Whatever you told him is safe with him, Sofia. He wouldn't betray your confidence like that."

Sofia rolled her head to face Eileen. "I'm sorry. I didn't mean it like that, exactly. It's just, I—" She wouldn't tell Eileen about their conversation or the kiss.

"Hmm." The older woman tapped her thumb on the serving tray. A gesture so similar to Nathaniel's that she knew exactly where he'd gotten it from. It made her miss him.

"Is he working late? Nathaniel, that is."

"He usually does these days, and I know he'll work himself to exhaustion until that Circle is finished. I wish he hadn't gotten involved. I know it's important to the town, but the schedule is too tight. It shouldn't be rushed just for a holiday. Families can picnic elsewhere for a few weeks."

Could his mother not know Nathaniel's true motive? "Why is Mrs. Reynolds so opposed to it?"

"I wish I knew." Eileen bit into a strawberry. "No one knows, and she won't say anything other than to get angry."

"People have asked her?"

"I have. Point blank, too. She's making my son's job harder, and I won't stand for that."

Sofia smothered a smile.

Eileen mumbled around another bite. "She just yelled at me about someone else."

Sofia traced the flower on her dress. "Was it April?"

Eileen's jaw dropped. "Nathaniel told you about his fiancée?"

Sofia nodded, pinning her lips closed so she didn't accidentally tell Nathaniel's mother that April had actually been his wife.

"Wow." Eileen set the tray aside. "He hasn't talked about April with anyone, including me, since she passed away a few years back. It utterly devastated him. They were inseparable those last years of high school, but after they graduated, I had no doubt she'd be my future daughter-in-law."

Sofia ached that this kind woman didn't know the truth, but after all this time, how could Nathaniel tell her?

"I suspected Nathaniel planned to propose that spring because he never did secretive well." Eileen shared a commiserative smile with Sofia. "The boy wears his emotion on his sleeve, as the saying goes."

Sofia chuckled. He'd shown her that side of him within the first few minutes of meeting her.

"He was jittery and snappish, and I knew an engagement ring burned a hole in the poor boy's pocket. He'd been working so hard that winter, picking up every snow job he could find. I worried for his health being out in all manner of cold weather."

She would have worried, too.

"Then one night, he comes for dinner. He's pushing food around his plate, and I knew something was on his mind. Without a word, he pulls this single solitaire ring from his pocket and tells us he planned to propose to April. My boy was all grown up and about to have a family." Eileen's voice cracked. "Then it was ripped away from him."

Words failed her, so Sofia reached over to grasp the older lady's forearm.

She looked at Sofia, eyes watery. "Is he… is he doing okay—now—with her loss?"

Sofia squeezed her wrist. "Healing, I think." And the Town Circle was part of that.

"Good. I—"

Eileen was cut off by a hail from a man who exited a newly arrived car. A nice one.

"That's Mayor Keller." Eileen stood and greeted him at the porch steps. "So glad you could make it."

"I'm not here for pleasure." Mayor Keller shook Eileen's hand. "I just finished a meeting with Mrs. Reynolds. She called for a stay of construction on the Town Circle and demanded your son's business be audited."

Sofia captured a gasp with her hand.

"What does that mean?" Eileen's hospitable nature fell away before her mama bear impersonation.

"Let's pray your son has all his affairs in order, or it could cost him his business. Either way, it will delay the construction. Mrs. Reynolds thinks it will allow the Town Circle to reopen as is, but it won't. All it means is that now we won't get to use it for the Fourth of July."

"Thank you, sir." Nathaniel hung up with his CPA and tossed his cell on the passenger seat of his truck. Dodger settled in the back seat now that he was off the phone. The poor dog panted like he'd gone without water for days any time Nathaniel took a call.

Nathaniel had nothing to fear from the audit, thankfully. *T*s would need to be crossed and *I*s dotted, but everyone knew this was a diversion technique. His CPA thought it doubtful the city auditor would give it more than a passing glance and that Nathaniel would be on track to finish on time as originally agreed.

And if the auditor looked more closely? His CPA assured Nathaniel that everything in his company was aboveboard and according to the books. Down to the contract with the city for the Town Circle, which had been looked over with a lawyer acquainted with his CPA. It was the 0.01 percent chance of things going wrong that still worried him. Somehow he suspected Mrs. Reynolds would find that single weakness and exploit it to her purposes.

The threatening rain clouds made it feel later than it was. Nathaniel could still drive over to his folks' place for the barbecue. He wanted to discover whether Sofia was there because if she wasn't, then he preferred to steer clear. She was the only person he felt like conversing with after the day's events. She understood better than anyone the stakes of this project. There was nothing he could do to keep April from leaving him, and now, it seemed he couldn't even beautify her favorite place.

He recognized the downward spiral he was slipping toward and rested his head against the steering wheel. *God, I can't do this alone. I'm tired of doing it alone. I don't know what You can do, seeing that You didn't take the cancer away, but can You please help me?*

The words felt like they bounced off the roof of his truck. He shoved it into gear and headed home. He wasn't in the mood for people and wouldn't risk driving by the Allens' to be disappointed when Sofia wasn't yet home.

Home.

He thought of the Allens' place as Sofia's home. It wasn't. She would only be there for a few more weeks at best. Unless she decided to find a place in River Cove and stay.

The idea lit a warm place in his chest that had been cold for too long. Still, doubts crowded in. Sofia admitted she was in no better place for them to be anything more than friends than he, and that's if her nephews even wanted to stay. What would it take to get all three on board? To have them around on a permanent basis? He'd get Sofia's permission before he slipped a comment to his mom, but Eileen Turner could have a list of everything Sofia would need to move here with the snap of her fingers.

Nathaniel eyed his phone as he turned off Main Street. He wanted to talk to Sofia, see if she was home and willing to talk. Then he spotted the dirt caking his arms and clothes. He'd shower first, then call her. Maybe he could invite himself over. Hang out with the boys before their bedtime. Then sit on the deck with her like they did the other night.

The thought soothed the sore spots in his chest, and he felt hopeful despite the challenges ahead.

He turned into the alley and parked behind the store. Dodger followed on his heels as he jogged up the outside steps to his apartment door. Dodger gave a happy bark, and Nathaniel stumbled to a halt. Sofia sat on the topmost step, waiting for him.

Her unruly curls fell about her round face as she smiled at him. She wore a purple sundress with bright sunflowers patterned across it. One foot encased in the boot, the other in a sandal. Sitting in the beam from the porch light, she looked like summer, and he wanted to drink her in. Instead, he offered her a hand and nudged Dodger out of the way as he helped her to her feet—well, foot.

"What brings you?" He thought he'd done a good job of asking it as casually as possible, but Sofia merely arched an eyebrow at him. Okay, he'd try another question. "Where are the boys?"

She didn't release his hand even once she was balanced on her good foot. "Mayor Keller told us what Mrs. Reynolds did. Your mom is watching Rowen and Tucker so I could wait for you here."

"You knew I wouldn't go to the barbecue?"

"Your mom did. Then I saw your truck at the Town Circle when I drove by, so I followed your mom's directions to your apartment. No need to talk in the open and potentially make things worse."

He should invite her inside. Offer her a glass of water or something. But he couldn't stop looking at her. She'd come here for him right when he needed her the most. Before he asked God for help. Was this the something? Was *she* the someone? It seemed he'd opened himself up to her whether he thought he was ready or not.

"Mind if we sit back down?" Sofia tugged as she lowered herself to the stair.

That galvanized him to action. "Why don't we go inside? It's dirty out here. What am I talking about? *I'm* filthy. Let me go clean up."

She tightened her grip on his hand. "Sit. Please."

Okay. He did as she requested. Dodger sprawled out on the landing behind Sofia, tongue hanging from the side of his open mouth as he panted. The scents of basil, oregano, thyme and sage swirled around them from his balcony pots.

"I don't want to leave the boys for too long,

not that they'd miss me." Sofia tucked a curl behind her ear. "They were having a blast. Met some other kids their ages. They barely acknowledged me when I told them I needed to run an errand."

"I'm glad. There's a good community here." He snapped his mouth shut. Was he sure he wanted to convince her to stay? Okay, yes, he was. But was it in *her* best interest? She was so consumed with doing the best for her nephews, he wanted to be the one to look out for her. Even if it meant pushing aside his growing desire to have her close by.

"I've noticed that," Sofia continued on, tugging his thoughts along with her, "which is why I can't understand Mrs. Reynolds's obsession with the Town Circle. I think there is something deeper going on."

"You're probably right." He realized her hand was still tucked in his and he ran his thumb over her knuckles. "But I can't get her to talk with me, and no one has been able to tell me whether or not they know what is eating at her, either. I've lived here all my life. You'd think I'd be able to figure this out. Why doesn't anyone know the story linking Mrs. Reynolds to the Town Circle?"

Frustration boiled, and at Dodger's nudge,

Nathaniel took a deep breath. The hint of manure wafted in from the farms surrounding River Cove, mixing with the smell of the coming rain. Sofia stretched out her booted foot, letting it rest on a lower step. He wanted to take away her pain, yet here she was helping him. It undid him, and he pulled free to rest his elbows on his knees, forehead on his palms.

"I would guess Mrs. Reynolds has a similar reason for her actions as why you wish to refurbish it." Sofia's voice was soft beside him.

"Loss."

"When my sister and I were kids, her favorite holiday was the Fourth of July. She loved the party atmosphere, the balloons, the fireworks, the barbecues, the parade. Even the man who dressed up as Uncle Sam on stilts."

Nathaniel lifted his head to pay better attention. Dodger scooted his nose against Nathaniel's side.

"When we were teenagers, we began helping with our church's float." She traced the petals of the fabric sunflower that lay over her knee. "Each year we enter a float into the parade as a way to participate in the community. Sometimes one or two of our musicians would perform, and sometimes it was just someone tossing candy—" up one petal, down the next, up and down "—but always there were tons of balloons and flowers."

"Flowers?" Is that why her dresses always had flowers? Or did he only notice the outfits that had a floral pattern because of his job?

"While not New Year's in California, our town made the July Fourth Parade one that showcased flowers." She shrugged as if it weren't a big deal. As a gardener, he loved the idea. "The goal is to have as much natural, living material as possible. The only caveat is that all the plants used must be planted around town afterward. It doesn't matter where as long as they are."

"That's a wonderful idea." Perhaps they could do something like that here in River Cove. They already had the parade structure in place. How difficult would it be to add flowers to the floats? He'd be happy to provide a list of retailers as well as give direction for planting the flowers afterward. He wrestled his thoughts back into the present. He wanted to hear Sofia's story, not revamp the town's parade. "Do you still participate in the float?"

"When I became the church administrative assistant, I took over our float. Anna helped with it every year. She was so creative about how to utilize the plants in a way that would allow for easy transplantation when the parade was finished. I have such fond memories." Sofia's voice trailed off, and Nathaniel's gut twisted. The math wasn't difficult to add up. Her sister passed away last fall, and Sofia was currently here in River Cove.

"What about this year? Will there be a float?"

"This year a volunteer is running it." Sofia's fingers bunched the fabric of her skirt, and Dodger wiggled closer to her. "It's the first year both Anna and I won't be at the parade in over two decades."

"I'm sorry, Sofia." He understood, deeply. Thunder rumbled in the distance. The storm would chase them inside soon. Dodger whimpered.

Sofia smoothed out her skirt and sat up straight. "Anything for Rowen and Tucker." She smiled bravely, but Nathaniel didn't miss the pain in her eyes. "I tell you that because Mrs. Reynolds must have a similar story relating to the Town Circle, and I aim to find out what it is."

What now? Nathaniel frowned. "Sofia, you can't get involved. This isn't your fight, and you don't need any more attention on you than what Mrs. Reynolds is already aiming to bring because of your association with me." Nathaniel's heart pounded at the thought. He rubbed Dodger's shoulder, the motion circling with his thoughts. The pain he could cause Sofia, adding to her grief. "No, no, I can't let you go anywhere near her."

Sofia's soft hand on his arm stopped its motion. Dodger wiggled. Nathaniel looked down. Dirt clung to his skin. He probably stank. Yet she'd touched him to comfort him. Not scolding or telling him how ridiculous he was being—and he knew he was acting foolishly because he had no right to order Sofia around—but he was afraid for her, and the fear was making him say things he didn't really mean.

"Nathaniel?"

He met her eyes, brown and warm and oh-so-close.

"We have to remember God hasn't turned a blind eye to us. It might seem like it when our lives look like the worn-down Town Circle. Loss makes things bleak and stagnant and..." Sofia chewed her lip and raised her eyes to the dark sky. They had only a short while longer before the rain forced them off his front stair.

Nathaniel wove his fingers through hers, grateful she didn't flinch at his dirty, work-worn hand. Dodger grunted and scooted away. Good dog.

"I can't help thinking that our lives are like the Town Circle, and if that's the case, then God is like you." She leaned into him. "His plan isn't to destroy it or make it some fancy life we hardly recognize. He wants to renew it. To bring life where there was none. To redeem what's been broken."

The words seeped into his heart like a gentle shower to dry soil.

"God is a gardener. A gardener of our hearts. Yours. Mine. Mrs. Reynolds's."

Nathaniel tugged his fingers free so he could wrap his arm around Sofia's shoulders, pulling her close to him. She smelled of lavender and vanilla and sunshine—a veritable balm to his heart. He rested his chin against her hair, the curls catching in his beard, and breathed. Each breath more deep than the one before, and by the third inhale, Sofia had relaxed, too.

Dodger panted behind them. Birds swept through the air, seeking shelter before the storm. A squirrel dashed into the parking area only to scurry back the other way. Lightning deep in the clouds flashed, revealing their billowing height.

For all the time he spent working outside, creating gardens for everyone else, how often had he sat still and enjoyed the outdoors—like the crackling anticipation of a summer storm—since April died? His parents invited him for casual evening walks to unwind, but he rarely took them up on the offer. The Allens welcomed him into their home, but he always found something to do there. And even his brothers hadn't given up on asking him to join them for one leisure activity or another. But no one succeeded in getting him to simply be until now.

He considered the prayer he believed God hadn't heard back in his truck on the way home, the one God answered even before he asked and answered more deeply than he could have hoped. Nathaniel was further away from refurbishing the Town Circle and honoring April's memory in time for the Fourth, but he finally had peace.

Chapter Ten

Despite the raindrops that dampened her shoulders, Sofia entered the Turners' church Sunday morning with a mission: she would speak to Mrs. Reynolds and find out what she had against the Town Circle being refurbished. Spruced up. Whatever word the woman wanted to put on it. Not destroyed or completely renovated. No, Nathaniel was renewing it.

She tried to ignore the warm sensation that washed down her back at the thought of his arm around her last night. They'd stayed in silence until the rain came, then she went back to the Turners' to pick up her nephews while he'd gone inside. It was a rare person with whom one could sit silently watching a storm move in, no need to force words or ignore any discomfort.

He also hadn't tried to kiss her again—not that she would have minded—but it wasn't the time or place, and even the kiss hadn't come between them. However, now it was simultaneously distracting and motivating her as she aimed to get to the bottom of why Mrs. Reynolds wanted to hurt Nathaniel. It was the least she could do.

She quickened her limping pace to catch up to her nephews, who'd already disappeared inside the sanctuary and were hidden by the many people gabbing instead of finding their seats. Longing thrummed through her. She could use someone to help her corral the boys, someone strong like Nathaniel. At the same time, being here in someone else's church made her wish to be back at her own church where she knew everyone and had a mission when weaving through a crowd. And she wanted this boot off!

A large purse knocked into her hip, pushing her onto her bad foot with more force than it could handle. Pain arched up her shin. She bit back a cry, wishing she hadn't left those stupid crutches at home. At the Allens'. Which wasn't her home. Oh, she was having a meltdown in the middle of a crowded foyer with no friendly faces and nowhere to go.

She stumbled again, this time into a man, and she braced herself by pressing her hand against the soft cotton fabric stretched across his broad back. She snatched her hand away before she fully had her balance. The man spun around and caught her arm before she tumbled. She recognized him instantly as Philip, Nathaniel's older brother.

"You're looking a little lost there." He flashed her a smile similar to Nathaniel's, but it didn't warm her like Nathaniel's did. He narrowed his eyes at her, then looked over his shoulder. "Your nephews already inside?"

"They're quicker than I am." Sofia's voice wobbled, and she cleared her throat. "I best go find them."

Instead of letting her go, or answering her, he glanced over her head and released a quick, sharp whistle. The kind that everyone hears, but is gone so quick, most would think they imagined it. Sofia almost thought she did, except that her cheeks grew inordinately warm.

"I'm used to wrangling kids—" he leaned toward her in a conspiratorial way "—so I'll go lasso those nephews of yours and leave you to my brother."

Before Sofia could quite comprehend what

Philip meant, he disappeared, and in his place was Nathaniel. He wrapped his arm over her shoulder and drew her toward a corner where she—and her foot—wouldn't be trampled.

She leaned back against the cool wall and breathed. Tears—a blend of humiliation, yearning and gratefulness—pricked her eyes. She willed them away. "I wish breaks would heal faster."

Nathaniel leaned a shoulder on the wall next to her, looking incredibly handsome in a blue button-up, rolled at the sleeves and showing starkly against his deep tan. "Reckon it's like that garden you talked about last night. Healing takes time. But have patience, Sofia. It will."

Hearing him say her name unlocked the sorrow pressing on her heart. "I miss my church." *I miss my job.*

He shifted so that he blocked her view of most of the foyer, cocooning them in this corner. "Have you talked to the boys about going back?"

"Not yet. I'm dreading it. I've dropped hints, and everything points to them having no interest in going home. They seem so happy and more like themselves than they have since Anna died." She waved her hands in punctuation to her words. "What if returning causes them to revert back to their sullen ways? Or worse?"

"You know you're always welcome here." Nathaniel's throat bobbed, as if he swallowed a whole sentence in one gulp.

When he didn't speak, she said, "I know, and if it's best for the boys, then I'll figure it out." Saying it aloud spread strength through her limbs. She could do this. With God's help, they'd make it through.

Nathaniel nodded, opened his mouth then closed it again. Did he not agree? Not understand?

"I have to think of them first, Nathaniel."

"I know, and selfishly, I want you here, too, so my interests and the boys' interests align, but I wouldn't be a good…friend…if I didn't worry about your interests and what's best for you."

Stunned, a spark of defensiveness shot through her. "Then why am I the only one that wants to go back home? I'm happy here, too, but I miss…so much. Why can't I just will myself to be happy if we stay?"

"Funny thing, grief." Nathaniel's phone buzzed and he glanced at it. "Phil has the boys, and they're sitting with my folks. You all right with that?"

Sofia nodded, her heart torn over the home she missed and the good people she'd found here.

Nathaniel pocketed his phone and tapped the toe of his black dress shoe on the gray-tone commercial carpeting, then he met her gaze. "Have you grieved, Sofia? I mean slowed down enough to let your heart break over Anna?"

Sofia clenched her jaw at the unnameable concoction of emotion welling inside.

Before she could express any of it, she spotted familiar gray hair past Nathaniel's biceps. It cleared her head and reminded her of her purpose this morning. She shoved her own troubles aside. She refused to focus on them at the expense of those around her. This morning she'd focus on Nathaniel. Then she'd figure out what to do about her nephews. Her own troubles would have to wait. Because the people she cared about needed her to put them first.

"Stay here." Sofia grabbed Nathaniel's wrist, yanking him out of the moment he thought they were having. He wanted to meet her in her grief, a place he knew all too well.

But, before he could reply, she limped her way straight over to Mrs. Reynolds and blocked the older woman's path into the church. Mrs. Reynolds squared her shoulders and raised her chin. His stomach plummeted. What was Sofia thinking? She was on an emotional edge—he recognized the signs of not facing grief because he'd been there— and she'd just walked straight into the fire.

The lights flashed, warning of the service beginning in a couple minutes, and the foyer began to empty. Not without many a backward glance at the two women staring at one another in the middle of the open area. It was like watching an old buck and new buck brace for battle.

He ran a hand through his hair. He wanted to get between them, stop Sofia from whatever she thought she was doing. However, he feared making the situation worse. Neither woman would welcome his interference in their *conversation*, even if he had no doubt it was about *him*. What could he do other than stand close enough to hear but far enough away that neither would think he was getting involved?

Anyway, what trouble could they get into before the service started in four minutes?

He edged closer, ignoring the side-glances and muttered comments fellow churchgoers cast at the women.

"I know who you are." Mrs. Reynolds raised a finger under Sofia's nose. "You're trying to replace April. Turning that boy's head. He has enough grief without you interfering."

Nathaniel felt himself turning red. Fortunately even more people passed through the double doors into the sanctuary, leaving fewer to witness his embarrassment. Not that word wouldn't travel like wildfire, even during the service.

"Loss." Sofia's voice was calm, almost detached. "I suspect you know something of it."

"Of what? Spinning men to your charms?" Mrs. Reynolds glared at Sofia.

"I lost my sister. Few months ago. She would have loved coming here for the Fourth of July to picnic on the Town Circle. The boys I have with me are hers, you know. I received custody of them after she passed. Brought them here to heal. Seems to be doing them good."

Nathaniel's gut twisted. Sofia shared a fragile part of her heart with someone who could use it against her, and doing so almost as if she were talking about someone else.

"What about you, Mrs. Reynolds?" Sofia cocked her head. "Who have you lost?"

"I'm not about to tell you."

"April, she was special to you?" Sofia met Nathaniel's eyes then, and he knew she recognized his presence, that he was there for her, if she needed him.

What would it look like for him to be by her side every day, in every situation? The idea called to him, but he shoved it away. For now. He definitely wanted to revisit the unnerving concept.

Mrs. Reynolds folded her arms, her large purse dangling from the crook of her elbow. "How dare you talk about April."

Sofia matched Mrs. Reynolds's body language. "You keep using her memory against Nathaniel. Seems you would only do that if she mattered to you. Otherwise, it's pretty cruel."

Nathaniel flinched. Mrs. Reynolds's expression became one of a cornered feral cat.

Sofia's eyes narrowed. "Who was April to you?"

Mrs. Reynolds grabbed Sofia's arm and yanked her down a hallway leading to the empty classrooms. "We will not discuss this where everyone can hear you."

Sofia winced as Mrs. Reynolds forced her

to keep up, but she subtly waved Nathaniel off from intervening. Nathaniel followed, however, keeping his distance until Sofia needed him. Music from the sanctuary chased them down the dark hallway.

"What do you know of April and me?" Mrs. Reynolds hissed, spinning Sofia so that she lost her balance and fell into a wall. Nathaniel lurched forward, but Sofia held up her hand.

"Nothing." Sofia steadied herself. "But you're going to tell me, and then the information will go no further than me. And Nathaniel." She nodded her head toward him, where he lingered several feet away.

Mrs. Reynolds went stark white. Nathaniel reached Sofia's side in a few steps. He guided her and Mrs. Reynolds into the empty classroom and closed the door against the music now filtering through the overhead speakers.

"You can't know," the older woman whispered. "No one is supposed to know."

"Know what?" Sofia prompted, sitting beside Mrs. Reynolds and tucking her fingers in the older woman's gnarled hand.

Mrs. Reynolds looked at Nathaniel, sorrow radiating from her. "April is my biological daughter."

Nathaniel stumbled away from her, his back hitting the closed door. "What did you say?"

Tears dripped from Mrs. Reynolds's eyes. "I had an affair almost thirty years ago and hid the pregnancy. I couldn't get rid of the baby, nor could I keep her, so I gave April to a younger mother I knew from church who struggled to get pregnant. The woman you know as April's mom."

Nathaniel's body trembled. April, his sweet April, was an unplanned pregnancy, an adopted child? He never knew. Did April know?

Perhaps he asked the question aloud because Mrs. Reynolds shook her head. "April never found out. I spent five months hiding in an extended-stay hotel in a Chicago suburb, since my husband asked for a trial separation. I thought I was alone until one of the housekeeping staff began leaving me encouraging notes after she cleaned my room. Eventually I wrote her back, and after months of correspondence, I finally arranged to meet her, and she showed me my way back to God."

Sofia rubbed Mrs. Reynolds's shoulder. "And you came back to watch April grow up?"

The older woman nodded. "I watched her

grow from a baby. Her toddling. Her imaginative games. Her prom." She turned an accusatory glare onto Nathaniel. "And now you're destroying her favorite place."

That galvanized Nathaniel enough to kneel before Mrs. Reynolds and take her hand from Sofia, though his still shook. "Are you absolutely telling me the truth?"

Her breath hitched. "How can you doubt me?"

He met her eyes, the room fading around him. "Because April and I married before she died." He gave her hand a little shake. "That's why I'm refurbishing the Town Circle. That's why this matters to me so much."

"You married my little girl?"

"And I loved her, Mrs. Reynolds. Surely you know how much I loved her." Nathaniel choked on the emotion clogging his throat. "I would have given anything to trade places with her."

"Oh, my boy." She cupped his cheek. "I wished every day that I would have told her the truth. That she would have known she had another mother who loved her."

Nathaniel squeezed his eyes closed, a tear slipping down his cheek. Small, cold fingers wrapped around his free hand. Sofia. She'd heard how much he loved April. He didn't regret it, but where would it leave them? Perhaps it showed the truth that his heart wasn't ready to move on, and it might never be.

"I don't understand." Mrs. Reynolds pulled away from him, but anger no longer laced her voice. "I never truly doubted your love for April, so why have you insisted on changing the Circle?"

Nathaniel freed his hands to wipe his cheeks, then sat on the other side of Mrs. Reynolds, where the older lady could block his view of Sofia. He couldn't look at her right now, couldn't risk seeing how she felt about him. He felt too vulnerable.

"Nathaniel?" Mrs. Reynolds patted his knee. "I'm genuinely asking this time. Why?"

He leaned forward, elbows on his knees. The gray tones of the room—light gray walls, blue and gray carpet tiles, gray folding chairs—all matched his mood. How could he help Mrs. Reynolds see his point of view? "I wanted to refurbish the Town Circle because it was April's favorite place."

"But why change it?"

"Why not make it even better?"

Mrs. Reynolds reared back. "I don't understand."

He grasped her hand again, willing her to see from his perspective. "I couldn't save her from the cancer, nor does anyone know my true relationship to her. I'm not her husband in the eyes of anyone, including her parents. I can't build a plaque or etch 'beloved wife' on her tombstone, but I can use my skills to make her favorite place beautiful."

Mrs. Reynolds patted their joined hands.

Nathaniel went on, not wanting her to speak. "How could I let her Circle crumble? For the lawn to grow worn with dirt and weeds? Not when I'm a landscaper. Her memory must be kept fresh and vibrant, like she was until the very end. Her smile was as bright and cheery as a pansy. Mrs. Reynolds, I know you hate this project, but please, will you let me finish it? I won't disgrace her memory."

Mrs. Reynolds gave a soft gasp, then collapsed in Nathaniel's arms, sobbing against his chest. Finally, he risked a look over at Sofia, who also had tears running down her beautiful cheeks. Something else shone in her eyes. Something that hit him in the rawest place of his heart. It wasn't pity or even compassion. She understood what he felt. More, she willingly shared in his emotion because she cared.

Chapter Eleven

Monday afternoon, Sofia sliced the third of three sandwiches into two triangles as the doorbell rang. The boys were playing out back, enjoying the sunshine after the rain. Nathaniel didn't ring the doorbell when he visited, and he never arrived this early in the day. Who else could be here?

She wiped her hands on a kitchen towel and limped down the hall, past the pictures of the Allens' family. She opened the door to find Mrs. Reynolds wringing her hands, rendering Sofia speechless. She still didn't know what to think of the story the older woman told them yesterday and hadn't had a chance to hear Nathaniel's thoughts, either. The service had ended by the time they'd all dried their tears, and then there were too many people, including her nephews, around to talk to anyone about anything that serious.

"I hope it's not a problem that I just stopped by. I didn't have your phone number, and I didn't want to ask Nathaniel. I've made a worse mess of things than I thought, and I hoped you would help me find a way to fix it."

"Of course." Hiding her surprise, Sofia waved Mrs. Reynolds inside. "Can I get you some of Mrs. Allen's lemonade?"

"If it's no trouble, dear." Mrs. Reynolds's eyes were red rimmed, and she wouldn't meet Sofia's gaze. In fact, the older woman looked a shell of the fierce fighter who'd dogged Nathaniel over the past couple of weeks. Despite their contentious beginning, Sofia couldn't help but feel compassion for her.

"Follow me, Mrs. Reynolds." Sofia led her to the outdoor table and settled her into a chair before she called the boys to get their sandwiches. When they begged to eat them in the hideout they were apparently constructing by the pond, Sofia let them so she could speak with Mrs. Reynolds without interruption.

The day was warm and humid, likely warning of another rain shower that evening. Perhaps blessing could be found in the mess Mrs.

Reynolds had created. The rain would benefit the sod, and Nathaniel wouldn't have to work in it. Sofia couldn't help but worry over knowing he worked out in the elements day after day.

Focusing on the task at hand, Sofia soon had lemonade and two sandwiches laid out on the table. Hopefully Mrs. Reynolds would like how she made it—turkey, lettuce, cheddar cheese and a light spread of mustard. It was how the boys liked theirs.

"Can you tell me what's going on?" Sofia settled in her own chair and propped up her aching foot on the chair kitty-corner to her. She hadn't needed the crutch all day, but walking too much at one time made the pain flare.

Mrs. Reynolds straightened her shoulders as she looked out over Mrs. Allen's garden. "I thought I could just tear up the stay of construction order so Nathaniel could return to his work on the Town Circle, but it turns out it isn't so easy." She turned to Sofia. "They have to finish the investigation I started, and even if they rush it, it won't be finished until the end of the week at the very earliest. That leaves only a few days for Nathaniel to finish the Town Circle before the Fourth of July."

"It's okay if it's not finished on time, right?" Sofia took her glass. With Mrs. Reynolds watching her so closely, she needed something to do with her hands. "Other than maybe disappointing the town." And she hated that for him.

"I didn't realize there is a clause in Nathaniel's contract that says he won't get paid the full amount if he doesn't meet his deadline. Each day past it means less money. It's a penalty that won't affect his or his business's standing in the community in any way—he's too loved for that—but it will cost him that money. I don't know how hard up Nathaniel is or how much he needs the money, and maybe he doesn't at all…"

Sofia toyed with a drip of condensation running down the side of her glass, thinking of the hopes Nathaniel had of expanding. Would he be able to do so if he didn't get the project finished on time and lost money because of it?

Mrs. Reynolds took a big breath, as if preparing to dive into the deep end of a pool. "I was wrong, and my actions are costing him. Oh, I warned him to stay away, and he didn't listen to me. I didn't want him mixed up with this. Then hearing about you, knowing he loved April, I lost my mind. And to think Nathaniel is my son-in-law. Even if he and I and you are the only people who will ever know. I can't sit idly by and allow him to suffer. Not knowing that. April would never let it happen."

Sofia's heart ached at the pain in Mrs. Reynolds's voice. She'd anticipated something deeply connecting the older woman to the Town Circle, but not this. Suddenly, Mrs. Reynolds reached across the space to clutch Sofia's free hand. Sofia quickly set down her glass to lean toward her.

"Sofia, dear, you were the only person I could think of to talk to about this. I don't know what you can do, but I know you care about Nathaniel, and you know both of our secrets. Please. Is there some way we can fix this?"

Sofia's mind scrambled. Tossing out scenario after scenario like a girl going through her closet to find something to wear for a first date. Finally, she arrived at a potential idea. "Do you think the people of your church and community would be willing to help Nathaniel? If we get enough volunteers, maybe we can make up for the lost time in a day or two."

"They would. That's not the problem. I'm

too embarrassed to ask." Mrs. Reynolds looked down at her lap. "And do you think he'd welcome that idea? What if he washes his hands of the whole project? Or he could hate overseeing people who don't have a clue what they're doing. It's a lovely idea, but—"

"He let my nephews help, so I don't see why he wouldn't welcome the volunteers." Sofia hated interrupting Mrs. Reynolds, but she needed to funnel the woman's energy into something positive. *I could use some help with that, God. You are in the business of redemption.* "And I don't see him walking away from this. It means too much to him. You, of all people, understand that. He'll see it through, no matter the cost."

That snapped her chin up. "I don't want it to cost him. I never have."

"I know, Mrs. Reynolds." She patted the wrinkled hand that gripped hers.

"I suppose I organized the protests, so I could organize volunteers. But what if people won't believe me, that I changed my mind? I can't very well explain why I've flip-flopped from being so against it to coordinating volunteers to save it."

"Maybe you don't have to." Sofia let the idea grow in her mind. Details and lists formulated without effort. "I do this type of thing all the time. It's my job. With you supporting me instead of protesting, and Mrs. Turner's connections, I'm sure we can pull this off."

"You'd do that for me? After everything I did and said? After what I put Nathaniel through? I know you love him, so I wouldn't be surprised if you hated me on his behalf."

"I—" Sofia's mouth wouldn't move. *Love him?* Surely not. "I don't hate you, Mrs. Reynolds."

The twinkle in her eye said she saw right through the diversion. "I noticed it plain as the sunshine yesterday at church. I can't imagine Nathaniel missed it, either. You haven't told him yet?"

"There isn't anything to tell." She didn't love him, right? They were friends. That's all.

Mrs. Reynolds frowned. "Why else would you be willing to work with his enemy—"

"You aren't his enemy, Mrs. Reynolds."

She waved away the words. "Fine, the sinful, hidden mother of his late wife, who everyone thinks is his fiancée."

Sofia couldn't stop the laugh from snorting out. She covered her mouth. "I'm sorry."

Mrs. Reynolds smiled, her shoulders relaxing. "I do suppose it's a rather convoluted mess. And yet you, young lady, are willing to wade right in." She pointed at Sofia. "You care about that boy—and don't deny it. You should tell him. Don't let time slip by without saying what you should. I know the pain of waiting too long."

Sofia glanced behind her to make sure the boys were still playing where she'd last seen them, safe and sound. The action bought her a moment to catch her breath as her mind tumbled over Mrs. Reynolds's exhortation. She had no idea what to say. Couldn't wrap her mind around whether the older woman's observations were true. She'd been worried about a summer attraction, but Mrs. Reynolds spoke of something deeper, something that could last. Had that type of…love…developed in so short a time?

From this distance, her nephews appeared fine, so she turned back to Mrs. Reynolds and ignored the topic completely. "I'll talk with Mrs. Turner, get her on board without sharing your secrets, then we'll make a plan and surprise Nathaniel with more help than he'll know what to do with." Then—and only then—would she, maybe, think about her motives.

Mrs. Reynolds smirked, then sobered. "Thank you, Sofia. I'm grateful God brought you here right when we needed someone like you. You are a blessing to this community, and I'm right sure I know at least one other person who would enjoy you staying around town once the summer is over."

Sofia knew Mrs. Reynolds referred to Nathaniel, but Sofia wondered whether Nathaniel truly felt that way. Yes, he'd kissed her, but then he'd pushed her right back into the friend category, a place she was content to be. Neither of them were looking for a relationship, nor were they in a place where they could manage one. She had her nephews to think of first, and Nathaniel…his heart still belonged to April.

Friday night came around too slowly. The past week, Nathaniel had mowed more lawns and gotten his business more organized than ever before—he'd need the money if he didn't meet the deadline—but he missed the landscaping side, and he didn't dare start any new projects until the decision came down about when he could finish the Town Circle. He thought he'd hear today, but now, at quarter to five, he guessed the answer wouldn't come down before Monday. More lost time.

He parked in front of the Allens' house and Dodger's tail got to wagging. Anticipation shot through him, too. The strongest bolt yet. It churned in his gut and warmed his chest. It unnerved him and energized him at the same time.

He'd finished work in order to arrive for dinner every night this week, something he hadn't done since April was alive, and he'd spent each night with Sofia and her nephews. He'd taught the boys about the garden, and they'd helped him mow the expansive lawn. Then there were the quiet evenings talking with Sofia about all their favorite summer memories. Sweet Sofia who listened to his stories, even the ones about falling in love with April.

In all that time, neither brought up the Town Circle, Mrs. Reynolds, nor whether Sofia would take the boys home once the Allens returned in two weeks. The very real possibility of losing Sofia loomed before him. The more he enjoyed her company, the bigger that fear became. He'd gone through it once before, and Sofia was the one pulling him out of the depths he'd fallen into. If Sofia left, where would he be?

Dodger barked, alerting Nathaniel to the presence of Rowen and Tucker moments before they mashed their faces into the passenger windows of his truck. He shoved the fear deep down where it wouldn't interfere with another evening with his favorite people. Only then could he laugh at the ridiculous expressions they created with their smooshed noses and splayed mouths.

He slid out and opened the back door so Dodger could greet his friends. The dog would miss the boys if they didn't live in River Cove, and the boys would miss Dodger. Maybe he shouldn't spend so much time with them only for them to leave. It would be hard on Tucker and Rowen. But he couldn't help it. What else was he going to do with his evenings but wish he were with them?

Then he spotted Sofia standing at the side of the house, hand shading her eyes. Yeah, there was no way he wasn't spending every spare minute getting to know her while he had the chance. *Just friends* was a bald-faced lie. He realized that over the last week. He'd come close to telling her, but he wouldn't until he knew whether she'd move her nephews to River Cove or not. He couldn't complicate her decision-making. Not when he didn't understand how he could let himself fall for a girl other than April.

"What ice cream did you bring today?" Tucker skipped alongside him as they headed to the house.

Rowen took the bag and peeked inside. "Fudge chocolate and strawberry."

Tucker whooped.

"Take it to the freezer for after supper." He pressed on Rowen's shoulder to send him ahead. He wanted to greet Sofia without an audience. His insides tumbled, sweat broke out on his neck and shame heated his face, reactions that had been growing worse each day this week. He shoved them away.

"Come on!" Rowen raced for the house, Tucker and Dodger on his heels.

Nathaniel forced a grin and shoved his clammy hands in his pockets. An attempt at a casual pose. Each day grew harder and harder to hold back on showing Sofia his affection. He told himself he wouldn't complicate her decision with promises of a relationship. In truth, he'd given up trying to know if he was ready for one after April. It seemed he must be, seeing that he couldn't get Sofia off his mind. Then why did this feel wrong, like he was betraying April? What if his heart was only repaired to enough of a degree that he could feel infatuation again? The thought of offering Sofia scraps of his scared and damaged self reinforced his resolve to wait.

"Fudge ice cream?" Sofia greeted him with a smile that cast sunlight on the cracks in his heart. "You spoil us."

She wore a light purple sundress that made her look like a sprig of lavender standing in a sea of green. He tried to find the words to tease her back, but his inner battle waged louder, and he couldn't get his head to send the right commands anywhere.

"Nathaniel?"

"Have you decided yet?" The words blurted out.

"About?" She looked genuinely confused. Of course she was. She hadn't been in his head for the last fifteen minutes.

"Sorry." Stuffing soil back into a bag was impossible, but he'd at least try to cover his blunder. "We can talk later."

"You look troubled. What's going on?" She was by his side now, and the last of his good intentions slipped through his fingers. He raised his palm to her cheek.

"Have you talked to Rowen and Tucker?"

"About?" The movement under his hand had him dropping his arm.

This was too much. He was confused. One

minute he wanted to be just friends and the next he wanted to crack open his chest to let the emotion pour out. He wasn't over April, so it wasn't fair to lead Sofia on. But Sofia breathed life into his dry soul.

"I should go home." Before he said and did something that muddled things up beyond repair. He shouldn't have visited every day this week. He shouldn't have gotten close to her or her nephews. He didn't do this kind of thing, and now he remembered why. If Sofia left, it would be like losing April all over again. And how he missed April.

"Nathaniel?" She caught his arm. "Talk to me. What's going on?"

He stared into her deep brown eyes. "I need—" He clamped down on saying anything more, knowing he'd blab everything in his head. About how beautiful she was. How he enjoyed being a person the boys could look up to. How he could see the four of them being a family. How all of that felt wrong because he was still with April. Except she was dead, gone, for years now.

"Aren't you staying for dinner and ice cream?" Hurt flashed before she could blink it away.

"I can't. Not tonight. I'm sorry, Sofia." He

ran for his truck and had already pulled away from the curb before he realized he'd left Dodger behind. He couldn't go back until he had time to simmer down or he'd make things worse for both of them

He rounded the corner before he pulled over and texted her: I'm sorry. I'll be back tonight. Can Dodger stay until then?

Sofia's reply was immediate: Of course. Are you sure you're okay?

Nathaniel's fingers shook, but he managed to type: Need to think. Tell you later.

He wasn't sure he would, but that's all he could think to say. He tossed his phone aside and turned toward the fields beyond River Cove. Down several country roads, he drove in silence, letting his brain meander without settling on one complete thought. Finally he came to the small pond where his dad often took him fishing as a boy.

He picked up his phone again and called Pops. "Hey, you up for fishing?"

"Right now?" The voice that taught him so much came through the phone.

"Yeah." Nathaniel tapped his thumb against the steering wheel.

"Our fishin' hole?" Shuffling came over the connection.

"That's the one."

Muted muffling, then, "Be right there."

Nathaniel whooshed out a breath as he leaned against the headrest. "Thanks, Pops."

Her nephews were not as disappointed about Nathaniel's unusual exit than Sofia was, but they were much more vocal about it. The three of them sat at the outside table like they always did for dinner, when the weather co-operated, but it didn't feel the same today as it had when Nathaniel joined them.

Not to mention, getting the boys to eat dinner without whining was a lost cause. And Dodger paced the deck like a caged animal. She'd be mad at Nathaniel if he hadn't looked so lost before he lit out of there like congregants leaving service for a potluck.

At least he said he'd return for Dodger. She would try to get answers from him then. He'd been willing to talk to her the past few evenings. In fact, it'd been wonderful, and she'd looked forward to the time after she put the boys to bed. Mostly they shared memories from their past. It was a safe topic. Not too deep, since she was not only afraid she'd blab about coordinating the volunteers, but she also couldn't bring herself to dig into the motivation Mrs. Reynolds had pointed out. She couldn't explore it, not when she needed her focus to be on her nephews. She'd said from the beginning she didn't have time for a summer romance.

"You both like spaghetti, and now it's getting cold." Sofia folded her arms. "Not eating won't make Nathaniel come back any faster."

"Why did he have to leave?" Tucker slumped in his chair. Dodger finally plopped down underneath, panting heavily.

She hated seeing her nephews disappointed. Why hadn't he at least explained to the boys why he couldn't stay? "I wish I knew, Tuck, but I don't have answers for you."

"You never do." Rowen stared out toward the garden.

"What's that supposed to mean?" Sofia let out a breath, immediately sorry for her sharp tone. She was frustrated with Nathaniel, not Rowen. "I'm sorry, Ro. Can you explain what you mean? I don't understand."

Rowen snorted. "You yank us here, and now you're yanking us back home."

"We haven't talked about going back home." She hadn't wanted to bring it up. Not yet. Not with how well things were going. But time wasn't on her side in that regard. The Allens would be back in two weeks and then…

"Not with us, you haven't. You never do. You don't want our opinions." Rowen rolled his eyes. "I heard you talking on the phone with Mrs. Allen. I know she's coming back soon, which means we'll have to go back to your stupid apartment."

Tucker's head whipped back and forth as he watched whomever was speaking, and Sofia felt like her heart was the ball being volleyed between them. She set down her fork. Her half-eaten spaghetti would go the way of the boys' dinners. Too bad Dodger couldn't eat it so it wouldn't go to waste.

Setting her own emotions aside, she folded her hands in her lap. "There is a lot packed into your statement, Rowen. Where can I start?"

Rowen pushed away from the table. "Are we staying or leaving?"

"I never said we would stay in River Cove longer than the summer."

Rowen flung his arms wide. "Then why don't we just go home now? I never wanted to be here in the first place."

"Then do you want to go home?" Sofia chewed her lip for a moment, praying for courage to ask the question she'd been stalling on asking. "Or would you prefer to stay here?"

"Is that an option?" Tucker bounced in his chair. "Staying here?"

"Rowen?" Sofia watched her nephew.

He seemed to battle something inside, then shrugged. "Like I care." Then he ran down the deck steps and raced past the garden.

"Did you mean that, Aunt Sofi?" Tucker ran a hand over Dodger's head. "Can we stay here?"

Sofia tore her gaze from Rowen's retreating form to look at Tucker and forced a smile. "I don't know, Tuck, but maybe. Obviously not in the Allens' home, but would you be happy living in River Cove?"

"I love this town. Dodger is here. And Nathaniel. And Mrs. Turner. And all sorts of nice people."

"What about back home?"

Tucker kicked his legs. "Mom won't be there."

Sofia coughed as if she'd just gotten a fist to the stomach. "I know, honey. But do you want to go back? It's okay if you do, even if you're sad about her not being there."

Tucker's young little eyes filled with unshed tears. "That's your house, Aunt Sofi. I miss my home. So I'd rather stay here in River Cove." Then he blinked the tears away, jumped out of his chair, patted his thigh and raced Dodger out to meet his brother.

Sofia buried her face in her hands. All this time she'd been thinking of what would be the best for her nephews, and she'd missed the most important thing. She hadn't given them a home that felt like theirs. How could no one have told her? She'd never done this before, taken in grieving children. How could she fix this? Besides moving—she was already considering that. If they moved, they might as well move here.

A sob caught her and she hiccupped. No matter what, doing what was best for her nephews meant giving up her home. Her home! And then it hit her, the full force of what that meant, and she realized why she hadn't been able to ask the boys about moving, why she hadn't been able to make a decision. It wasn't about the boys at all. It was about *her*.

She'd have to give up the place where she and Anna had concocted so many plans. Where Anna first told her about dating *this guy*. Wedding plans. Burial plans. The number of tears Anna cried on her sofa as Sofia tried to comfort her after she lost her husband.

Sofia had lived in the same condo her entire adult life. She'd bought it after college with the money given to her after her parents passed away. It wasn't large, but it was packed with memories, many of which she'd shared with Nathaniel this past week. She understood Mrs. Reynolds now. Her anger and stubbornness about changing even a blade of grass on the Town Circle.

She thought about Nathaniel running away from her earlier. He'd said something about Sofia's decision whether to stay in River Cove. Was that the reason he couldn't face her? She recalled his observation of her on Sunday, asking whether she'd grieved Anna. Sofia hadn't wanted to answer him. She'd avoided the pain by masking it with taking care of the needs of everyone else.

Now her time had run out.

Chapter Twelve

Nathaniel sat in one of the camp chairs his dad brought, fishing pole held loosely in his hand. Pops sat next to him. The only difference between them was that Pops had a soda in his free hand. Mom never allowed soda at the house, but she stocked it for Pops's fishing trips.

The sun wouldn't set for a while, but the breeze cooled the warmth of the day. Gnats hovered and a bullfrog croaked. The water of the small lake spread out as still as glass. Nathaniel wished he could share such a perfect moment with Sofia, but she was the reason he was here with Pops in the first place.

"We've been sitting here near an hour and not one fish." Pops grunted. "Ya going to start talkin', or is this going to be a wasted evening?"

Nathaniel chuckled. Of course Pops knew that the real reason Nathaniel asked him to join him at the fishing hole had nothing to do with the fish. The problem was, Nathaniel still didn't have the courage to tell Pops what he needed to talk about. Because he first needed to tell him about April. And if he told Pops, Pops would tell Mom. And hurting Mom was the last thing he wanted to do.

"This have something to do with that pretty gal with the two nephews?"

"Kinda." Nathaniel tugged his line to make the bobber dance in the water.

"Spit it out, son. No need to talk around the barrel or explain the whole process to me."

Nathaniel couldn't stop a laugh. He'd said much the same thing to Sofia when she'd first mentioned possibly moving to River Cove. Ironic.

Pops grunted again.

"I think I'm in love with Sofia." His face burned from the admission, but it felt good to say the words aloud. This would be the perfect kind of place to share those words with her. He glanced at Pops for his reaction.

"*Hmph!* I could've told you that. I'm not blind, son."

"What about April?" The words felt wrung from his core.

"What about her? I know you loved her."

"Did you know I married her?" He didn't mean to blurt it out quite so harshly.

Pops methodically set his soda can in the chair's holder and his fishing rod on the ground before turning to face Nathaniel, hands clasped in his lap. "Why did you hide it, son?"

"April—"

"After she died. Why not tell us then?

Nathaniel shook his head. "I couldn't do something against her wishes." He met his father's gaze, grateful for the lack of anger or disdain—not that he'd ever looked at him that way. "I'm sorry, Pops."

The older man cocked his head and considered him, making Nathaniel squirm under the scrutiny. His father's lack of judgment heaped guilt on his shoulders. Should he have told his family after April died? Probably. But his grief had been so intense, so strong, he couldn't have thought of what would be best for anyone. He'd barely had the capacity to remember to eat. After the funeral, at which he was *only* the fiancé, he'd thrown all his energy into his work. It wasn't until the past few days that he'd slowed down enough to enjoy dinner with someone else multiple times in the same week. And look what slowing down got him: heartache.

Pops took a swig of soda. "What made you tell me now, son?"

Nathaniel flexed his shaky fingers against the rod he still held. "I told Sofia about April."

"Then what's the problem?" Pops frowned, his first negative emotion. "Or has she turned away from you because of this secret?"

"No." Nathaniel rubbed his chin. "No, it's not her at all."

"Then what's all this?" Pops swiped his hand to encompass Nathaniel, sloshing soda inside the can.

Nathaniel squared off. He needed the answer to this question; it's why he'd asked to go fishing. "Pops, am I ready for a new relationship?"

"Hogwash." Pops slipped his soda can in the holder and rested his elbows on his knees before staring Nathaniel down like he hadn't done since Nathaniel was an unruly teen. "No one—do you hear me, no one—is ready for a relationship the first time 'round. We learn by doing, by trial and error, by loving and forgiving. Why would the second be any different?"

The words struck Nathaniel like gravel spray.

Pops squinted. "What's really keeping you from telling Sofia you love her?"

Truth? "Her boys."

Pops sat back. "You don't want to be a dad? I'm surprised. You and April—"

"It's not that. Though you saying it has me sweating." He tossed a smile his dad's way. He set the rod down so he could fist his hands to hide his shaking fingers. "Sofia doesn't live here."

"So?"

"So one of us would have to move. Thing is, she thinks the boys would do well here."

Pops swatted at a bug. "I don't see the problem, son."

"Sofia would give up everything for them. She would lose her home, her job, her friends and community."

"And gain you."

Nathaniel dropped his chin. "I'm not worth all that, Pops."

A Cheshire grin spread across Pops's face. The proverbial cat got the canary. It froze Nathaniel because whenever Pops got that look—and at this magnitude, *phew-ee*!—Nathaniel was in for a sermon of epic proportions. But this is why he'd called his dad, right?

"Son." Pops rested his palms on his knees. "When you see an empty lawn or a cracked patio, ya don't look at it with those eyes. You're a landscaper so all you can see is potential. In that there brain God gave you, you create a design that's fit for the customer and, above all, brings life and beauty to an otherwise barren place."

Nathaniel couldn't help but nod. It was all true. And he enjoyed it.

"Now, when you plant those little seeds of yours, you leave enough space for them to grow. Ain't that right? Because you see the finished product and plant with that finished design in mind."

This sounded good and all, but… "My worth isn't in my work, Pops."

"That ain't my point, son." He wagged his finger like a preacher man. "This is what you need to hear. God has promised to make all things new. Your worth is in Him, and He has planted you exactly where you need to be. Not because of who you are now, but with your future in mind."

Nathaniel hitched a breath as the truth of Pops's words slammed into him, repeating the verse Sofia had shared with him the other day.

"Now. I know you love April, but, truth is,

she's gone to Heaven. She's happy. Time you should be, too. My advice is to tell that new young lady what's in your heart. She needs to know if she's supposed to make a well-formed decision. Moving here doesn't have to mean her loss. Now get on outta here. Go tell her how you feel. I'll clean up—" he winked "—after I give the fish one more fighting chance."

"Thanks, Pops." Nathaniel forced the words past his choked throat.

Pops shooed him, then grabbed Nathaniel's rod and settled back in his chair with both poles in the water.

Nathaniel took in the scene as his father's words settled in his soul. He slapped his thighs. It was time to tell Sofia exactly what was on his mind. He rose, fished his keys from his pocket and patted his dad's shoulder as he passed.

"Love you, son."

No matter what happened, Nathaniel could bank on one truth: both his earthly father and Heavenly Father loved him. That gave him the courage to find out whether Sofia loved him, too.

Sofia paced the deck for the third time, then sat to rest her foot, only to jump up and pace again. Gratefully the sun wouldn't set for another hour yet. At this rate, it would take her that long to get down to the pond to get her nephews' attention. They were set on ignoring her, even with her shouting the promise of ice cream. She stalled, however, hoping Nathaniel would return for Dodger before it got too late.

Her foot ached, and as the minutes passed, she realized she'd have to go to the pond herself. She considered bringing her crutches but decided on using only one since she couldn't balance with both on the uneven lawn. With a prayer for help, she limped down the deck stairs and struck out for the back part of the Allens' property.

She made it to the garden before the reality of the situation struck her. Her foot already hurt, and she hadn't even made it a third of the way to the boys. It would ache something fierce by the time she got to them, then she'd need to manage to get herself all the way back to the house. She patted her pocket, assuring herself she had her phone with her, should she need help. A little more at ease, she continued on her trek past the garden.

Her nephews spotted her as she passed the last row of vegetables. They'd built a triangular structure made of sticks. Dodger ran up to greet her, but her boys didn't move. Teeth clenched against the growing pain stabbing the top of her foot, she worked her way all the way to the pond. Each step and the boys' eyes grew wider and wider.

"Wow, Auntie, I didn't think you could get way out here," Tucker said as she reached them.

Sofia couldn't say anything past the pain that now burned up her ankle, so she sat on the damp grass and breathed hard. Sofia wiped her forehead, realizing sweat gathered there. Her ears buzzed, and not because of all the gnats and mosquitoes out here.

"Whatcha doin'?" Tucker scooted next to her, Dodger beside him, but Rowen crossed his arms and rested his back against the fort.

"Why didn't you come to the house when I called you?" She clenched her jaw, angry at herself that she let the pain harden her words. Good moms shouldn't—but she wasn't their mother. Right?

Tucker ducked his chin. "Rowen said not to. But I wanted ice cream."

Tears stung her eyes. Why was this so hard? "Tuck, are you supposed to listen to Rowen or me?"

"I want to listen to my mom." Tucker's lowered chin wobbled.

That sliced through her anger, shame and pain to strike at the most tender place in her heart. She cleared her throat to keep the tears at bay and pulled Tucker in for a hug. "She asked me to look after you because she wanted me to take care of you. I can't do that if you don't listen to me."

"Okay." Tucker tilted his head from side to side. "Is Nathaniel coming back?" Just like that, he accepted her words, hopeful joy returning to his little face. Her own heart couldn't keep up.

"Dodger is here, so he'll be back sometime." She reached to pet the dog's head, then looked over at her other nephew and braced for their conversation. "How about you, Rowen? Why didn't you come to the house when I called?"

"Didn't want to." He folded his arms, his face the picture of a storm cloud.

She squeezed the cushioned handle of her crutch as if it could keep her emotions steady. "Rowen, honey, please talk to me."

His jaw worked for a moment before the words tumbled out. "Why can't you marry Nathaniel and we could all live here and be a big happy family?" He seemed to realize what he'd said, clamped a hand over his mouth, jumped to his feet and raced for the house. Dodger barked and raced after him. Sofia could only stare at the retreating pair.

Tucker bounced beside her. "I love that idea! Auntie Sofi, do it! Let's be all one big happy family!" Then he ran after his brother, leaving her alone as dusk turned the sky pink overhead.

Sofia bent her good knee so she could hug it. Bugs circled her head. If she stayed much longer, she'd be eaten alive. But the boys' words stunned her. Yes, she had her answer to what the boys wanted. They missed their home, and hers alone wasn't enough. They wanted a family, with a mom and dad, not an aunt.

She laid her forehead on her knee. Why had God taken Anna? She's who the boys needed. Sofia couldn't be their mom. She hadn't even known her house wasn't the home they needed. And now, instead of immediately calling a real estate agent to put her condo on the market and moving them to River Cove, like she should if she was the person they needed her to be… Sofia's heart broke over what she'd be leaving behind.

Hadn't she said she'd do anything for the boys? Funny how those words only served to keep Nathaniel away from her heart, which had evidently failed, too, considering the hurt his leaving had caused her today. So was she really willing to do anything, sacrifice anything for her nephews? Was she willing to give up her job, her home? Was she willing to risk her heart to live in the same small town as Nathaniel?

What if she told the boys they were going to have to make it work back home, away from Nathaniel? Would they act out even worse? If only she knew the right steps to take and the best way to help them. Administrating things was so much easier. She knew the tasks that needed to be done, the number of people she needed to accomplish it, and even when problems arose, they were managed with the same attention.

Take the volunteers for the Town Circle. They were aiming for Monday, if Mrs. Reynolds could pester city officials to release them to work on the project by then. So far, Nathaniel didn't know. The whole town had managed to keep it a secret. Or maybe someone had let it slip and Nathaniel thought she'd interfered? Perhaps that's why he'd run away this afternoon? She might have to use that favor he'd mentioned one of the first days they met in order to even get him to the Town Circle on Monday.

The cold ground seeped through her dress, and the mosquitoes left welts on her arms. Why hadn't she grabbed a sweater before hiking out here? She needed to get back to the Allens' house, but all her energy had been spent. She tried to summon the last dregs to push to her feet, using the crutch as leverage, but the mental battle was too much, and she sank back to the grass.

If only she could call Anna and ask for advice. She'd know exactly what Sofia should do. Just when Sofia lost her best friend, she had to make the biggest decisions of her life. If Anna were here, what would she say?

Turn your worry into prayer.

Was that idea from Anna or Eileen Turner? Either way, Sofia decided she had nothing to lose by taking their advice. She let out a long breath and prayed.

Nathaniel parked in front of the Allens' house. His pulse pounded as he anticipated seeing Sofia again. He'd need to apologize first. Then he aimed to tell her exactly how he felt, just as Pops had suggested. Where they went from there, they could hopefully figure it out together.

It was strange arriving at the Allens' without Dodger. The darkening evening made it more difficult to see, but he strained his senses to pick up on his dog's presence. Dodger had to be outside. Somewhere.

The lights were still on inside, so Nathaniel walked around back. No Dodger. No Sofia. No boys. Unease skittered up his back. He was wrong to have let his emotions get out of hand. He shouldn't have left.

He tapped lightly on the patio door, then slid it open. He heard a sharp bark, and Dodger raced toward him from the den. One mystery solved.

Nathaniel rubbed him down. "What are you doing inside?"

Dodger circled, then led him to where Rowen and Tucker had fallen asleep on the couches. Nathaniel dug out blankets from the ottoman and covered them.

"Where's Sofia?" he asked Dodger. There was no sign of her in the house, but she wouldn't have left the boys alone. He remembered the first day they met, how he'd struggled to give her the benefit of the doubt.

Now he knew she'd do anything for her boys, which meant something prevented her from getting the boys to bed up in their rooms. Something like her foot?

Instead of going upstairs or even to another part of the house, Dodger nosed the patio door. Nathaniel slid it open, and Dodger darted off the deck. The unease that had lessened when he found Dodger and the boys turned into full-blown worry. Surely Sofia hadn't ventured past the garden with her foot in that boot. Was she stranded somewhere, unable to get home?

Dodger turned in a circle before dashing into the growing darkness. Nathaniel grabbed the flashlight Mrs. Allen kept in one of her kitchen drawers and followed Dodger as he pulled out his phone to call Sofia's number. It rang twice before someone answered it.

A sniffle, then Sofia's voice finally said, "Nathaniel?"

"Thank God. Where are you?" He should have greeted her, apologized or something else, but his relief at hearing her voice was too great.

"By the pond. I only have a little battery left on my phone because I've been using it as my flashlight. My foot isn't holding up, and

Tucker wasn't strong enough to help me, so I sent him back to the house with Dodger. Oh, wait, Dodger is here? Where are my boys?" He detected an edge of panic in her voice.

"They're asleep inside." Why hadn't she mentioned Rowen? Surely both boys working together could have provided the help she needed. Regardless. "Stay put. I'm coming to get you."

Night settled, and this far from any larger town, no light pollution brightened the sky. No moon or stars out tonight, either. The powerful beam of his flashlight cut through the darkness and illuminated his steps. Never had he been more aware of the divots and bumps in the expansive lawn. Dodger met him at the back edge of the garden, and Nathaniel raised his flashlight to find Sofia.

"Nathaniel!" She waved from ten feet away.

She leaned on a single crutch, the toe of the boot just off the ground behind her. She slid the boot forward, and attempted to step with her good foot, only to cry out and nearly tumble. Nathaniel was at her side in a few steps. He couldn't stop himself from grabbing her shoulders and inspecting her for any injury besides her foot.

"I'm okay." Her voice shook. "A little scared and my foot...hurts."

He swept her into his arms. The boot pulled her leg down against his forearm, and the crutch hung from her hand. "What are you doing way out here at this time of night? Strike that. You can tell me later. Are you sure you're okay?"

She rested her head against his shoulder. "I don't know what I am, honestly, other than glad you're here." She took a ragged breath. "I've made a mess of things. Rowen is so upset, he wouldn't let Tucker talk him into coming out to help me. I can't say I blame him. I'm afraid I lied to myself about all I'm willing to sacrifice for the boys."

"Do they want to move to River Cove?" He walked slowly, stretching their time together, giving her a chance to talk and him time to hold her in his arms. He made a mental note to have a conversation with Rowen about his behavior. Whether it was his place to do so or not, Rowen couldn't treat his aunt that way.

"They don't feel at home in my condo. They need a space that is ours, not mine."

"I can understand that. My apartment feels more like a torture chamber some days. I guess I stayed because I felt I deserved it."

Sofia lifted her head. "Nathaniel, you don't deserve that. Your time with April, all those memories you shared with me this week, are a precious gift." Her voice choked. "I feel like I'll lose mine if I move."

Nathaniel tightened his hold on her. Here he was trying to comfort her, and yet her words were a balm to him. She didn't resent April or his past with her. Sofia understood. She shared in his grief, and it was one of the things he realized he loved about her. They'd reached the edge of the garden, the deck steps not far away. He wanted to tell her about his own revelations that evening but knew tonight wouldn't be that night. First she needed to grieve and heal, but he could be there for her, just as she was for him.

"You can always share your memories of Anna. Maybe sharing them will help you remember, no matter what home you live in."

She relaxed in his arms, and he hoped that meant she appreciated his offer.

As he climbed the deck steps, he added, "You know you can always call me."

"But you left," she said, hurt evident in her tone.

"I know and I'm sorry. I'll tell you about why, I promise." He laid her on the deck lounge chair. "The boys are sleeping on the sofa inside, so let's have a look at your foot before we wake them."

She nodded but bit her lip.

As gently as he could, he tore the Velcro strips apart, starting at the top. She winced with each one but whimpered when he pulled at the last one. And then her tears began falling.

"What's wrong? What—" He turned the beam of the flashlight on her foot. It was swelling by the moment. "I'm going to get ice and call Dr. Bradley. Stay here."

She curled into herself, rocking in a self-soothing kind of way. He couldn't take away this pain, but he could get her help.

"Sofia, sweetie, I'll be right back. Hold on."

In the time it took to get the ice pack and one of Mrs. Allen's quilts, he'd gotten a hold of Dr. Bradley. He laid the quilt over her, covering her bare arms—which had multiple bug bites—then settled the ice pack on her foot. She hissed, but didn't fight it. Then he pulled a chair close to her head, held her hands with his one hand and caressed her curls with the other.

Emotion swelled as he was transported to April's hospital room. How many hours, days, had he sat like this by her side? Sofia wasn't dying, but she was in pain, and here he was again. He tightened his hold on her hands. It was time to say goodbye to April, to give her to God whose side she was now at, healthy, whole and as vibrant as ever. His place was here now, with Sofia.

Once she worked things out with her nephews, he'd support her decision, whatever it may be. If that meant leaving River Cove, as long as he was by her side, that is what mattered. Through it all, he planned to show her he loved her. Until she was ready for a relationship, until she was ready to be more than friends, he would wait and love her patiently. Then when it was time, he would tell her.

He ran his thumb over Sofia's pain-wrinkled brow. If only he could take away her pain.

His phone vibrated in his pocket—he'd turned the ringer off after calling Dr. Bradley. He freed it to see the caller ID, surprised that Mayor Keller would be calling him at this hour, and answered.

"Good news, Nathaniel. You're cleared to begin work again on the Town Circle Monday morning."

Nathaniel gaped. Of course that's why the

mayor would be calling, and after Mrs. Reynolds's revelation on Sunday, he wasn't surprised everything worked out, but somehow he wasn't expecting the news at this particular moment in time.

"Nathaniel, did you hear me? You're in the clear. The audit and all the paperwork are done."

"Yes." Nathaniel cleared his throat. "Thank you."

"We awarded this project to you because you're one of our own. We knew you would handle it appropriately, and we believe you have and will continue to do so. I look forward to seeing it completed in a timely manner."

"About that, Richard." Nathaniel swallowed, knowing his next words would cost him. "The week delay—it's my fault I didn't build in any buffer. I won't make the July Fourth deadline. I know there will be penalties involved—"

"Which we can waive."

"But the community picnic and Fourth of July Celebration. It won't be ready. The lawn will be, since the sod should have taken by now. But—"

"Nathaniel, do you believe in the residents of River Cove?"

"Yes…" He drew out the word, unsure what the mayor meant.

"Good. Then give that gal of yours a kiss of thanks and be ready to go first thing Monday morning."

Nathaniel stared at his phone, realizing the mayor had hung up on him. Obviously Sofia was the *gal*, but did everyone think they were a couple? And why did Mayor Keller say that Nathaniel should thank Sofia? The kiss part was obvious, but what did she have to do with the Town Circle?

Could Keller be thinking of the way Sofia confronted Mrs. Reynolds at church last week? Sofia did deserve a kiss of thanks for that, but the townspeople would never know the true extent of Mrs. Reynolds's connection with the Town Circle, nor how close it was to Nathaniel's reasons for refurbishing it. Could he be honest with the town? Tell everyone, including April's parents—adoptive parents— what he'd told his own dad tonight?

Dodger scrambled down the deck steps as the sound of a car reached Nathaniel. Dr. Bradley, likely. Perhaps he'd test the waters by telling the good doctor, then tomorrow, he'd tell his mom and brothers, in person. If he was still standing, he'd visit April's family and tell them the truth.

He wished Sofia could be by his side when he did, but she needed to rest after overusing her foot tonight. And this was something he needed to do alone, to put his past behind him, so he could explore the future he and Sofia might have together.

Yes, she definitely deserved that kiss of thanks. For whatever reason Mayor Keller thought, sure, but mostly because she'd helped Nathaniel face his grief and his secrets and pulled him into the light of a hopeful future. In all honesty, Sofia Russo deserved many thankful kisses, and he couldn't wait to bestow each one.

Chapter Thirteen

Morning sun woke Sofia. She pried her eyes open. Her foot throbbed, sending pulses through her whole body. She rolled over and realized she lay on the Allens' den sofa, covered with a quilt, which brought back some of last night.

For as much as her foot currently ached, it didn't hurt as bad as last night. Even so, it hurt much worse than when she'd first injured it. The pressure under the skin, after Nathaniel removed her boot last night, felt like it would cause her foot to explode. The ice pack Nathaniel had gently rested on the injured area helped instantly, she remembered that much, but it had still taken all the energy her tired mind could spare.

After that, her memory fogged, leaving her

to latch on to what she did know. She could picture Nathaniel there for her, taking care of anything that needed doing, including keeping watch over her nephews. Speaking of her nephews—she sat up—where were they? The house was oddly silent, and she felt the distinct lack of people.

She scrubbed her hands over her face. At some point last night, Dr. Bradley arrived, and Nathaniel moved her to the couch inside. The vague memory answered why she was currently covered with a quilt on the sofa in the den. Dr. Bradley said some things she couldn't recall. Though she did remember him encouraging her to take pain medicine before he left. What happened next? Where were her nephews?

She swung her feet to the floor, her foot protesting the movement. Her mouth felt full of cotton, and the space between her ears didn't feel much clearer. Coffee would help. Then she spotted the note on the ottoman, held in place by a small round tray with a glass of water and a small vase holding a single yellow flower. She wished she knew what kind it was, but it looked like a daisy. She tugged the note free.

Took the boys to work in the garden. Call
or text me when you wake up.
—Nathaniel

Sofia flopped back on the sofa, enjoying
the warmth that wrapped around her. When
was the last time she felt cared for? Throughout the last months, she'd been caring for everyone else. Her job at the church majored
on service—and she loved it. Her care of the
boys had been singularly focused—at the expense of caring for herself, she realized now.
And standing up to those who thought her
grief should have expired…that was exhaust-
ing. Now, this one person—a handsome one
at that—had made her the focus of his care,
and she felt so…loved?

That's why she couldn't reconcile the man
who'd carried her to the house last night with
the one who ran away from her earlier the
same evening. Not to say she didn't like this
new Nathaniel. He seemed open with his care
for her, which made her positively giddy for
the surprise awaiting him once he received
the all clear to return to work on the Town
Circle. She grabbed her phone, needing an
update.

Instead of letting him know she was awake,

she called Mrs. Reynolds. She sipped her water while she waited for the older woman to answer.

"Any news on whether Nathaniel will be able to resume work on the Town Circle?" she asked with little preamble after Mrs. Reynolds's greeting.

"He should hear any moment—or maybe he already has—that the stay has been lifted, and he can get back to work on Monday morning." The older woman gave a dignified squeal. "And I have another surprise up my sleeve. I can't tell you what it is, but I think you'll be pleased."

Joy and curiosity mingled as she hung up with Mrs. Reynolds. Next she called Dr. Bradley, needing a refresher on his diagnosis. As the phone rang, she prayed that she hadn't rebroken her foot. She took another sip of water, her throat dry again at the thought.

"You were out of it last night." The doctor sighed. "My professional opinion is exhaustion mixed with pain combined to knock you off your feet. A good thing, in my mind. The body knows best. You've been on your foot too much without the crutches, and it reaggravated the fracture. If you don't stay off of it, we might have to talk surgery because it won't heal properly. Now, you let that young man, well, all three of those young men, take care of you for the next week. Be sure to ice it and take your pain meds—Nathaniel put them in the cabinet next to the sink, second shelf where the boys can't reach them—and then we'll *talk* about taking you off the crutches again."

Somehow, as reprimands went, Dr. Bradley's felt more like encouragement. Hope. The future had seemed so dark and unknown, but now, with people around her who cared and supported and helped…what was she to be scared of?

She slipped on the boot, wincing at the new swelling that hadn't gone down yet. Her next conversation caused the trepidation to inch back, so she sent up a prayer asking God to open her nephews' hearts so that they would be willing to listen to what she had to say.

First she would apologize, then she would ask for their cooperation. There was trust she needed to build with them, not as the fun aunt, but as their mother figure. She couldn't straddle the line any longer, no matter how much she hated the idea of stepping into Anna's shoes. She'd told the boys last night that Anna gave them to her, had tasked her with caring for them in her stead. It was time to take hold of that mantle.

She spotted her crutches leaning against the edge of the sofa, waiting for her. She hopped over to them, then situated them under her arms. It felt like a setback—it *was* a setback—but in her heart, it seemed like a huge step forward. She had a community of people she could lean on, she knew that now. Though whether that meant moving to River Cove was the answer, they'd have to see, but for the first time, leaving her condo didn't sting quite as much as it had before.

She slid open the patio door and instantly spotted all three of her favorite people. Tucker threw a stick for Dodger. Rowen lugged a bucket of something through the garden. And Nathaniel stood watching them, hands on his hips, feet and shoulders squared off. He stayed when she needed him. Just like he stayed for April.

Last night's running away was the anomaly. Nathaniel Turner didn't run when faced with hard times. Tears didn't scare him. Injury. Death. So what sent him running last night? He'd promised to tell her, and she desperately wanted to know.

Nathaniel issued an instruction carried

away on a stiff breeze. Humidity hung thick and clouds obscured the sun. Birds chirped. Squirrels chattered. No rain dampened the deck, but it would only be a matter of time. Likely the weather didn't help matters with her foot.

She stepped onto the deck. The thump of her crutches must have caught Dodger's attention because his head turned in her direction. Then his tail started going as if it was the motor to wind him up and shoot him across the yard. His sudden burst turned three other heads her way.

Tucker raced after Dodger. Sofia turned her hip as Dodger nearly crashed into her. Tucker skidded to a stop in front of her.

"I'm sorry for not listening, Auntie Sofi." The words tumbled out. "I know you only want what's best for us, and I promise I'll try to listen as if you're my real mom."

"Oh, honey." Sofia grabbed a chair to sit on in order to be at Tucker's level and wrap him in her arms. "All is forgiven. Will you forgive me, too, for not listening well enough? I love you so much."

Dodger nosed in, and Tucker laughed. "I love you, Auntie Sofi."

Tucker and Dodger bounded down the

steps. Sofia looked over the deck railing in time to see Nathaniel rest a hand on Rowen's shoulder. The young man looked up at Nathaniel and nodded solemnly. Nathaniel gave a one-armed hug, then sent him toward the deck.

Sofia's heart pounded as she waited. What had Nathaniel said to the boys?

"Aunt Sofia?" Rowen didn't meet her eyes as he toed the wooden slats of the deck. "I'm sorry for not listening to you and not helping you last night."

"You're forgiven." She reached for his hand to draw him closer. "I'm sorry for not listening, too. Can we work together to figure this out?"

Rowen's chin lifted an inch. "I miss my mom, and I don't like that you're not her."

Sofia shoved the tears back. "Me, too. I wish she were here. She made a much better mom than I could be."

Rowen's head bounced up, his brown eyes meeting hers. "That's not true. You'll be a great mom. I always wanted cousins. Maybe Nathaniel could be my uncle."

Sofia bit her lip to stop a smile. "In the meantime, your mom gave you to me. That means I have to be like your mom."

"I know, that's what Nathaniel told me. I'll try to remember." Rowen scuffed the toe of his shoe, again. "Tucker wants to call you mom. I—"

"Don't have to."

His eyes widened. "You mean it?"

"Of course." She squeezed his hand. "What you call me won't change how much I love you."

He gave a crooked grin. "I guess I love you, too." He shrugged.

"Get on with you." Sofia laughed.

Rowen bounded down the steps, passing Nathaniel as he made his way to the deck, and Sofia didn't miss Rowen's loud words. "Your turn. Don't mess this up."

Nathaniel grinned as he reached the deck. "I like those two."

Sofia tried to relax, but so much needed to be said between her and Nathaniel, she didn't know where to start. She searched his face, looking for any clue where she stood with him. "Thank you for talking to them."

Nathaniel pulled up a chair beside her. His eyes were kind, his shoulders at ease. "I understood where they were coming from, so we bonded over breakfast. Also told them I'd take them fishing, if you don't mind."

"Of course not." Sofia chewed her lip. The wait was killing her. Did she ask the questions or wait for Nathaniel to spill the answers?

"Look, Sofia, I'm sorry I left without explanation yesterday. I was scared. And ashamed." He rested his elbows on his knees. "April—she will always be a part of my past. I didn't know if I could have a future without her. Then you came along." He cleared his throat. "I have more I want to say, but not yet. First I want you to know that I care about you, that I plan to support your decision on moving to River Cove or not. And that you can always call on me, no matter what."

"Nathaniel?" Sofia tugged her skirt hem closer to her knees. "It sounds like you're breaking up with me. But we're just friends, right?"

"Are we?" His bold gaze took her aback.

"Friends?" Yes, of course they were friends.

"More than friends?"

Her heart thumped. This was it. This was her chance to say yes. To step into a future where she would always have someone beside her. Someone who cared about her like Nathaniel did.

He held up a hand. "I promised myself I wouldn't ask that yet, but here I am breaking my promises already." He rubbed his neck. "Before you answer that question, I have some things I need to clear up with other people close to me. It's time—" the corner of his lip disappeared between his teeth "—everyone knew April was my wife."

Sofia's heart broke for him, and she grazed her fingers across his knee. "Do you want...? I don't know what I can offer, but I'm here for you, too."

Nathaniel glanced at where she touched him. "I received word that I'm back to work on the Town Circle Monday morning. I'd enjoy it if you and the boys would be willing to join me."

"You can count on that. We'll be there." With a crowd of volunteers in tow.

Nathaniel placed a kiss on her cheek and was gone, calling for Dodger to join him and taking her heart with him.

Monday morning turned out to be a perfect weather day for Nathaniel to work outside. Bright sun, rain-washed air, cool breeze. A few clouds and not a hint of humidity. Then again, everything looked brighter knowing he'd see Sofia in an hour. Truth be told, that was the most exciting part of his day. Sure, he looked forward to getting back to landscaping, but the Town Circle didn't have the hold on him it did even a week ago.

Nathaniel gathered his supplies into the bed of his truck, settled Dodger in the back seat and started the engine. The past two days he'd worked at repairing the relationships grief had broken. Everyone seemed to take the news that he and April had married relatively well. April's parents promptly declared they were changing her grave marker and welcomed him as their son. He debated telling April's mom that he knew about Mrs. Reynolds but decided to let that secret lie until Mrs. Reynolds was ready to tell it.

Pops hadn't told Mom like Nathaniel thought he would, but instead of being hurt like Nathaniel expected, she demanded to know what he was doing about Sofia. His brothers also focused on Sofia, asking whether he'd proposed yet. Well, today began his plan to win her heart, to convince her that they should be more than friends. He had all the time in the world to convince her, though he hoped she wouldn't make him wait too long. With his heart feeling free for the first time in years, he itched to kiss her again.

The Town Circle appeared much the same

as when he'd left it a week ago, except for the sod that looked ready for its first mowing. He'd wait until the night before the Fourth of July Celebration so at least it would be perfect. The front trellis arch and pond were both built and ready for plants. The photo arbor, on the other hand, was an empty space that had no chance of being ready in time.

Nathaniel let Dodger out of the truck and grabbed his own water bottle and a hoe, mentally organizing his plan for the day. First he'd inspect the trellis and pond area to make sure they'd held up as they should have. Then he'd prep the photo arbor before running out to the garden center to claim the plants for the trellis and pond. He'd plant those tomorrow, then finish the arbor after the holiday.

He jiggled one of the supporting beams of the entrance trellis. It held soundly. Dodger ran ahead of him. Nathaniel circled the pond area. Other than leaves and standing mud water that he'd need a pump and Shop-Vac to clean out, the outer stones held beautifully. Tomorrow he'd fill it with fresh water.

He walked over to the photo arbor next, and his heart sank at the mud puddle. Dodger's bark interrupted his disappointment, and he looked up as the dog raced across the lawn.

Sofia had arrived. His heart took a definite uptick. Even if the Town Circle wasn't ready by the Fourth, he wanted to spend the holiday with Sofia and the boys. That's what mattered.

He left the hoe and water bottle and jogged toward them. No way would he let Sofia traverse the grass without a hand ready to catch her if she wobbled. He'd brought a camping chair for her, too.

"What can we do to help?" Tucker shouted from the welcome trellis as he ran toward Nathaniel. Dodger leaped beside him. Joy and energy poured from both of them.

"Do you need more of your stuff?" Rowen yelled, pointing over his shoulder at his truck. The conversation they'd had the other day endeared the grieving young man to him. He was glad Rowen had chosen to speak honestly with his aunt, and he'd promised him he'd always be a listening ear if Rowen needed a man's advice.

"Grab the camp chair," he called back to Rowen. Then his eyes fell on Sofia.

She navigated the stone walkway under the arch, her crutches under her arms and a smile on her face. Today she wore a loose T-shirt and dark-wash shorts, plus the ever-present boot. He quickened his pace, meeting her just inside the arch.

"Hi." He grinned like a schoolboy, but he didn't care. In that moment, Nathaniel wanted to take the day off and spend it with her. Who cared about the Town Circle, anyway? Not when this beautiful woman was here with him.

A car pulled into the parking area, stealing his attention. Mrs. Reynolds. Why was she here? Would she protest again? Did she want to help? Sofia stiffened beside him.

A second car parked beside his truck. He'd recognize his mom's sedan anywhere. And then his dad's truck and his brothers and the pastor and... Nathaniel yanked his ball cap off his head as he realized the line of cars stretched down the road.

"What's going on?" Nathaniel glanced at Sofia. Of course she didn't know, either. Or did she? The hesitantly searching look on her face made him wonder. "Do... Do you know what's happening?"

Sofia's grin grew. She wrapped her arm around his, pinning the crutch between them. "They're here for you, Nathaniel. We're going to get this Town Circle ready for the Fourth, and we're going to do it together. The whole community."

"What?" His brain scrambled.

Her face fell. "You're happy, aren't you? Mrs. Reynolds wasn't sure, but I thought—"

"Mrs. Reynolds helped?" He stared at Sofia.

"And your mom. I coordinated it. That's okay, isn't it?"

"You did this for me?" She did this for him? "When?"

Sofia's shoulder lifted beside his arm. "Mrs. Reynolds visited last Monday, and we hatched the plan with your mom."

"You didn't say anything all week." How had she—and the whole town—managed to keep this from him?

"That's the point of a surprise." She pulled away from him. "You're not happy. I'm sorry, Nathaniel. I thought—"

"You amazing, incredible, lovable woman." Nathaniel wrapped his arm around her waist, knocking the crutches aside, and kissed her in front of God and the entire community— who'd apparently come today to help him finish this project, all thanks to Sofia.

The kiss, however, was cut short, not by the whistles he knew came from his brothers, but by Sofia's phone. She ignored it until it rang a second time in the universal signal that someone immediately needed to get a hold of her.

She smiled apologetically as she answered. Nathaniel kept his arm around her since he had no intention of letting her go until she knew exactly how he felt, only a hundred-fold now. This woman was the one for him. He just needed to know how to tell her, how to show her, that he was willing to sacrifice for her just like she was willing to do for everyone around her.

He watched in amazement as person after person filled the Town Circle, all dressed ready to work. Did he have jobs for all of them? Who cared! If each person planted a flower, they'd be done in minutes. He'd have Philip be in charge of supplies. Simon could handle gathering a lawn mower and edgers. His mom would coordinate food—she always did—and his dad could bring over the benches he made.

Sofia's gasp yanked him away from his mental planning.

"Heidi," she was saying, "you can't just give up. There are spare balloons—yes, I know it's only two days away. Heidi—" She looked at her phone. "She hung up on me."

His brows tugged downward. "What happened?"

Instead of answering, she scrolled through

her contacts for Pastor Flores. She leaned against Nathaniel while she waited for the other man to answer, her breathing short and quick. Something was obviously wrong.

"Hi, Pastor, I just heard from—yes, that's what she told me, but I can—no, sir—yes, sir—I understand—thank you. You, too." Sofia sagged and Nathaniel lowered her to the ground.

Within a moment, they were surrounded. Her nephews were there, his brothers, his mother and a ton of other nosy neighbors, but Nathaniel did his best to make them give her breathing room.

"What happened, Aunt Sofi?" Tucker squatted at her side and voiced what they all wanted to know. Had there been another tragedy?

She took Tucker's hand. "Honey, your mama's float won't be in the parade this year."

"We weren't going to be there to see it, anyway." Rowen crossed his arms, but Nathaniel didn't miss the hardening of his chin. This mattered to him, too.

Tucker's lower lip trembled. "But just because we aren't there, you promised they'd still have the float. We can fix it, can't we?"

"I'm sorry, honey. Pastor Flores said they

wouldn't be entering the float." She smiled bravely, but Nathaniel didn't miss the grief in her voice. "But we'll be here. We can celebrate with River Cove. Doesn't that sound fun?" She looked at Nathaniel then, eyes pleading that he help her. She could count on him, and he had just the idea.

"This float, would you like to build one here?" he asked, looking from her to the boys. "One with balloons and flowers we plant afterward?"

At Sofia's soft intake, he knew she caught his reference—that he had, indeed, been listening as she told him about the float she held so dear.

Rowen's eyes widened. "We could do that here?"

"Here in River Cove?" Tucker clapped.

Tears welled in Sofia's eyes. Nathaniel squeezed her hand and turned to find Mayor Keller among the community volunteers.

"What do you say, Mayor?" he asked when he spotted the man standing behind Philip. "We already have a Fourth of July parade that runs from Town Hall to the Town Circle. Let's add flowers to all the floats, then plant them here in the Circle when the parade concludes."

Chattering rolled through the crowd.

"I like it." Mom voiced her opinion first. His brothers and Pops seconded it. Other voices joined in.

Mrs. Reynolds raised a hand. "I have something I need to say, first."

Nathaniel helped Sofia to her feet so he could hold her as they listened.

"April Kinder, Nathaniel's April, loved this park." She coughed into a tissue. "I spoke with her parents this week, and with the mayor, and we have a gift for Nathaniel, for all his work to create a better place for our community." Mrs. Reynolds waved someone over.

The crowd opened to allow April's parents to walk closer, holding a board between them. When they reached Nathaniel, they flipped it around to show the words engraved on its front: The April Kinder Town Circle.

Tears clogged his nose, and Sofia tightened her hold around his waist.

Mrs. Reynolds dabbed the tissue under her eyes. "I'm sorry for the trouble I have caused the town, but especially Nathaniel. He is a good man who loved April."

Should he tell everyone about his true relationship with April?

Before he could decide, Mrs. Reynolds continued, "The reason behind my actions is because I loved April, too." She glanced at April's adoptive parents. "You see, April was my biological daughter."

Whispers darted through the crowd, and Nathaniel stepped to Mrs. Reynolds's side. "Mrs. Reynolds isn't the only one with a secret. April and I married before she…" He couldn't finish. But instead of feeling alone in his grief, he recognized Sofia's hand on his shoulder and the presence of his family and his community pressing close.

Mrs. Reynolds gripped his wrist. "I'm sorry for the pain I have put you through, Nathaniel. I ask your forgiveness, but I understand if you cannot give it."

"Of course I forgive you." He hugged the older woman, the woman who he now knew was his late wife's biological mother. "How can I withhold forgiveness when we both have been grieving for so long?"

Mrs. Reynolds blinked away her tears, and a smile showed through.

Nathaniel reached back to draw Sofia closer to him. "What better way to christen this new park than to plant flowers—which I have ready—after a parade celebrating what makes us a community? All in favor of a Fourth of July Flower Parade, say *aye*."

A chorus of *aye*s went up, and a few hats, too.

Sofia laughed beside him, and Nathaniel bent down to grab a kiss that tasted of sweet tears. His heart overflowed with love and memories and hope for a future that must include Sofia and her nephews.

"Does this mean you might stick around River Cove after the Allens return?" He shouldn't ask now, in front of everyone, but he couldn't hold back the question any longer.

"Yes, yes, lets!" Tucker bounced beside them.

"Please, Aunt Sofi?" Rowen gave her a nudge. "You know what else I think?"

"Hush." Sofia turned the deep red of a spring tulip.

Rowen widened his eyes at Nathaniel, sending him a message that had Nathaniel tugging Sofia out of the circle of neighbors. Though not away from their prying eyes.

"Sofia, whether you choose to stay in River Cove, move back to your home or go across the ocean, I want to be by your side. Not as a friend. As more. I love you."

"This…" Her brown eyes turned glassy

as she waved toward all the people watching them. "This support is what I've been looking for, and I would be honored to join this community."

Excited chattering grew around them, but Nathaniel ignored it, holding hope that Sofia would give his heart the other answer he desired.

"And I want to be by your side. But I'm a package deal, Nathaniel. Two rambunctious boys. Are you sure?"

Yes, he loved Rowen and Tucker. "I already care for them as if they were my own. I'm very sure."

Tears dropped down her cheeks. "I love you, Nathaniel."

"And I love you." He kissed her again, the promise of a vibrant future blooming before them.

Epilogue

One Year Later...

The sun warmed Sofia's shoulders as she shaded her eyes, looking for the start of the annual River Cove Fourth of July Parade. Her nephews would be riding in the second float, with Pops at the wheel of the tractor that pulled Simon's hay wagon. The boys had worked all week with Nathaniel and his brothers to create the farm-themed display, and none of them let Sofia peek.

The Town Hall bell rang at nine o'clock, and Sofia grabbed Nathaniel's arm. "Here they come!"

Nathaniel's laugh rumbled through her. She was so proud of him. His business had boomed once he'd completed the Town Circle. After she'd moved the boys to River Cove, they stayed with Mr. and Mrs. Turner until an old farmhouse became available. Nathaniel helped her and the boys begin fixing it up, and she couldn't help hoping that one day Nathaniel would ask her to join their little family, and become her husband and a father to her boys. Meanwhile, she took the position as his administrative assistant, and she thoroughly enjoyed working beside Nathaniel, helping his business succeed.

She raised up on tiptoes, her height a disadvantage at events like this. She wouldn't get in front of the kids who lined the road to the renamed April's Circle, but their parents needed to squat a bit lower.

"There." Nathaniel pointed. The mayor rode in an old-fashioned, roofless car and waved to the crowd. Beside him sat Miss River Cove, a young high school student who won the position at the end of the school year for outstanding efforts in building community. She'd teamed up with Sofia and Pastor Flores to coordinate donations for the women's shelter near Sofia's old church, and Sofia couldn't be prouder.

"That's them!" Sofia bounced. She freed her arm from Nathaniel's and waved at her boys. They'd blossomed here in River Cove.

The Turners welcomed them into the family like long-lost relatives. Pops and Eileen were grandparents to them, Philip and Simon were uncles and Nathaniel filled a father figure role.

"You're going to wear yourself out before we get to the planting part." Nathaniel chuckled.

She grinned up at him, relishing how he looked at her with such love in his eyes. "Mrs. Reynolds's house is going to look so pretty when we're done."

He wrapped his arm around her waist. "She deserves it, don't you think?"

After revealing her connection to April, she'd become the Circle's biggest advocate and Nathaniel's loudest cheerleader. Sofia knew Nathaniel would always have a soft spot for the older lady, and the two of them had become close because of it.

The parade rumbled closer, and Sofia got her first good look at her nephews' float. "Wow! You boys outdid yourselves!" Her nephews were dressed like two scarecrows standing amid loose straw. Dodger barked beside them, his tail flinging pieces everywhere. Hanging from the sides were window boxes full of flowers showing every color of the rainbow.

Rowen and Tucker pointed at Sofia and waved as they jumped up and down. Sofia grinned at them, her heart overflowing. Nathaniel let out a whistle. And then the parade continued on down to April's Circle.

Nathaniel grabbed her hand. "Come on. We can beat the mayor's car and get the best spot for when they arrive."

He tugged her through the crowd, and they hurried up the street. Sofia laughed as she attempted to keep up. Her foot only ached before the harshest of storms these days, but mostly she forgot she ever broke it. Except that it helped to bring her and Nathaniel together.

They arrived, just a little breathless, at the back of the Circle. All the flowers they'd planted after last year's parade had filled in and were blooming in gorgeous fashion. Sofia especially loved the photo arbor, and it was there that Nathaniel stopped.

Sofia pressed a hand to her chest. "I haven't moved that fast since the boys were little."

A slow smile lit Nathaniel's eyes.

Before she realized what he'd done, Nathaniel lowered her to the two-person bench beside him. In front, a row of stones, stacked three high, created a barrier between the arbor and the rest of the Circle. Behind stood a trellis wall of vines and flowers. Sofia didn't know their names, but the flowers were purple and pink and white. It created a cozy cove of nature.

"I love this place." Sofia rested her head on Nathaniel's shoulder.

His arm came around her, and with his other hand, he raised her chin. "You're happy."

"Very happy."

A worried crease appeared between his eyes. "No regrets about moving here?"

"What made you ask that? We moved almost a year ago." Sofia sat up. "What's going on? You're being—" Her jaw dropped as he slid off the bench and onto one knee. She covered her open mouth. "Nathaniel?"

His throat worked as he gathered her hands in his. Then he met her gaze. "You brought hope and joy back into my life. This past year with you by my side is something I want for as many years as God grants us. I love you more than anything, Sofia Russo. Will you marry me?"

Nathaniel held his breath, waiting for Sofia's answer. He was pretty sure it would be yes, but there was always that tiny chance, that piece of him that worried this was all too good to be true. He would spend every day of his life proving to Sofia how much he loved her. He loved her nephews, too. That's what he forgot to say in his proposal! He wanted to say he thought of them like his own sons.

Before he opened his mouth to amend his proposal, the breeze loosened one of Sofia's black curls, and he reached out to caress it away. Sweat dripped down his back. What was taking Sofia so long to answer?

Now she grinned at him, her eyes sparkling with tears, and—wait—was she laughing at him?

"What? Do I have something on my face?" He ran his palms over his beard, which he'd trimmed just for this moment. "Oh! The ring." He patted his pockets. He was making a mess of this.

"Nathaniel, stop." Sofia was fully laughing now. "You were so lost in making sure you said the right thing that you missed my answer. And your sweet face was so worried." She trailed her finger down his cheek.

"Your answer." He stilled. "I missed it?"

She nodded. "I said *yes*."

Nathaniel bounded to his feet with a whoop. He lifted Sofia off the bench and spun her around. This woman wanted to spend the rest of her life with him. How God had blessed him!

He set her feet on the ground so he could pull her close and kiss her.

"Did she say yes?" A boy's voice cut in, followed by a dog's bark. "Did she? Did she?"

Sofia grinned against his lips before she turned to her younger nephew. Straw dangled from his sleeves and his floppy hat was missing. "Yes, Tuck. I sure did."

"Yippee! I get a mom and a dad!" Tucker leaped in the air, Dodger jumped and barked with him. Then together they raced away like pinballs, with Tucker telling every person he bumped into the happy news, a line of straw in his wake.

Nathaniel didn't blame him. He wanted to do the same thing.

Rowen approached, a smile lighting up his freckled face. He'd grown several inches the past year, so it hadn't been hard to find a pair of pants with legs too short for his costume. Nathaniel treasured the solemn talks he had with the boy as they fished together—Tucker couldn't sit still long enough, so he rarely joined them. And while Rowen hadn't shed all of his grief, his humor showed up more and more.

Now his eyes twinkled as he waved Nathaniel's cell. "I got a couple pictures, just as you asked. Figured you wanted a kissy one."

Nathaniel tightened his hold on Sofia as she giggled. Forget the picture. He wanted another kiss. Instead, he thanked Rowen and pocketed the phone, only then realizing it didn't bump against the ring box that should be in his pocket. Panic sliced through him. Where had he left it?

"Looking for this?" Rowen held out the velvet box, and Nathaniel sighed with relief. "It fell out when you gave me your phone earlier. No time to give it back."

"Thank you!" Nathaniel opened it to reveal the simple solitaire he'd chosen. He showed it to Sofia. "What do you think?"

She beamed at him. "I think this is the beginning of a wonderful life together."

He pulled her close, visions of the future dancing in his mind. Of bringing Sofia fresh-cut flowers. Of more fishing chats with Pops and Rowen. Of harvesting produce with Tucker and any other children they might have. Of long summer nights spent with the woman he loved. He pressed his lips to hers. Yes, a flourishing future together indeed.

* * * * *

Dear Reader,

Thank you for reading Sofia and Nathaniel's story. I'm thrilled to join the Love Inspired family with this debut. A huge thank-you to all who helped bring you *A Father for Her Boys*. There are many names I could list, and I thank God for each of you.

Grief appears in many forms. I pray my attempt at portraying that blesses your heart with the promise of God's presence through those difficult times and the hope of Him making "all things new" (Revelation 21:5). While I cannot claim to have Nathaniel's green thumb, I have been in Sofia's "boot," needing to wear one after suffering a stress fracture in my foot. I've also known the challenge of being laid up with a sprained ankle as a mom of little boys, and I'm glad I could put those real-life experiences into the pages of this story.

Thank you again for reading *A Father for Her Boys*. I'd love to keep in touch! Visit my website, daniellegrandinetti.com, to sign up for my newsletter and find my social media links. If you enjoyed this story, would you consider leaving an honest review on your preferred retail site? Reviews are a great way to help support your favorite authors and their books.

I'm grateful to have readers like you.

Danielle Grandinetti

Get 3 FREE REWARDS!

We'll send you 2 FREE Books plus a FREE Mystery Gift.

FREE Value Over **$20**

Both the **Love Inspired®** and **Love Inspired® Suspense** series feature compelling novels filled with inspirational romance, faith, forgiveness and hope.

YES! Please send me 2 FREE novels from the Love Inspired or Love Inspired Suspense series and my FREE gift (gift is worth about $10 retail). After receiving them, if I don't wish to receive any more books, I can return the shipping statement marked "cancel." If I don't cancel, I will receive 6 brand-new Love Inspired Larger-Print books or Love Inspired Suspense Larger-Print books every month and be billed just $6.49 each in the U.S. or $6.74 each in Canada. That is a savings of at least 16% off the cover price. It's quite a bargain! Shipping and handling is just 50¢ per book in the U.S. and $1.25 per book in Canada.* I understand that accepting the 2 free books and gifts places me under no obligation to buy anything. I can always return a shipment and cancel at any time by calling the number below. The free books and gift are mine to keep no matter what I decide.

Choose one: ☐ **Love Inspired Larger-Print** (122/322 BPA GRPA)   ☐ **Love Inspired Suspense Larger-Print** (107/307 BPA GRPA)   ☐ **Or Try Both!** (122/322 & 107/307 BPA GRRP)

Name (please print)

Address   Apt. #

City   State/Province   Zip/Postal Code

Email: Please check this box ☐ if you would like to receive newsletters and promotional emails from Harlequin Enterprises ULC and its affiliates. You can unsubscribe anytime.

> ### Mail to the Harlequin Reader Service:
> **IN U.S.A.:** P.O. Box 1341, Buffalo, NY 14240-8531
> **IN CANADA:** P.O. Box 603, Fort Erie, Ontario L2A 5X3

Want to try 2 free books from another series? Call 1-800-873-8635 or visit www.ReaderService.com.

---

*Terms and prices subject to change without notice. Prices do not include sales taxes, which will be charged (if applicable) based on your state or country of residence. Canadian residents will be charged applicable taxes. Offer not valid in Quebec. This offer is limited to one order per household. Books received may not be as shown. Not valid for current subscribers to the Love Inspired or Love Inspired Suspense series. All orders subject to approval. Credit or debit balances in a customer's account(s) may be offset by any other outstanding balance owed by or to the customer. Please allow 4 to 6 weeks for delivery. Offer available while quantities last.

Your Privacy—Your information is being collected by Harlequin Enterprises ULC, operating as Harlequin Reader Service. For a complete summary of the information we collect, how we use this information and to whom it is disclosed, please visit our privacy notice located at corporate.harlequin.com/privacy-notice. From time to time we may also exchange your personal information with reputable third parties. If you wish to opt out of this sharing of your personal information, please visit readerservice.com/consumerschoice or call 1-800-873-8635. **Notice to California Residents**—Under California law, you have specific rights to control and access your data. For more information on these rights and how to exercise them, visit corporate.harlequin.com/california-privacy.

LIRLIS23

Get 3 FREE REWARDS!

We'll send you 2 FREE Books _plus_ a FREE Mystery Gift.

FREE
Value Over
$20

Both the **Harlequin® Special Edition** and **Harlequin® Heartwarming™** series feature compelling novels filled with stories of love and strength where the bonds of friendship, family and community unite.

YES! Please send me 2 FREE novels from the Harlequin Special Edition or Harlequin Heartwarming series and my FREE Gift (gift is worth about $10 retail). After receiving them, if I don't wish to receive any more books, I can return the shipping statement marked "cancel." If I don't cancel, I will receive 6 brand-new Harlequin Special Edition books every month and be billed just $5.49 each in the U.S. or $6.24 each in Canada, a savings of at least 12% off the cover price, or 4 brand-new Harlequin Heartwarming Larger-Print books every month and be billed just $6.24 each in the U.S. or $6.74 each in Canada, a savings of at least 19% off the cover price. It's quite a bargain! Shipping and handling is just 50¢ per book in the U.S. and $1.25 per book in Canada.* I understand that accepting the 2 free books and gift places me under no obligation to buy anything. I can always return a shipment and cancel at any time by calling the number below. The free books and gift are mine to keep no matter what I decide.

Choose one: ☐ **Harlequin**
Special Edition
(235/335 BPA GRMK)

☐ **Harlequin**
Heartwarming
Larger-Print
(161/361 BPA GRMK)

☐ **Or Try Both!**
(235/335 & 161/361
BPA GRPZ)

Name (please print)

Address   Apt. #

City   State/Province   Zip/Postal Code

Email: Please check this box ☐ if you would like to receive newsletters and promotional emails from Harlequin Enterprises ULC and its affiliates. You can unsubscribe anytime.

Mail to the **Harlequin Reader Service:**
IN U.S.A.: P.O. Box 1341, Buffalo, NY 14240-8531
IN CANADA: P.O. Box 603, Fort Erie, Ontario L2A 5X3

Want to try 2 free books from another series! Call 1-800-873-8635 or visit www.ReaderService.com.

COMING NEXT MONTH FROM
Love Inspired

THE TEACHER'S CHRISTMAS SECRET
Seven Amish Sisters • by Emma Miller

Cora Koffman dreams of being a teacher. But the job is given to newcomer Tobit Lapp instead. When an injury forces the handsome widower to seek out Cora's help, can they get along for the sake of the students? Or will his secret ruin the holidays?

TRUSTING HER AMISH RIVAL
Bird-in-Hand Brides • by Jackie Stef

Shy Leah Fisher runs her own bakery shop in town. When an opportunity to expand her business comes from childhood bully Silas Riehl, she reluctantly agrees to the partnership. They try to keep things professional, but will their past get in the way?

A COMPANION FOR CHRISTMAS
K-9 Companions • by Lee Tobin McClain

When her Christmas wedding gets canceled, first-grade teacher Kelly Walsh takes a house-sitting gig with her therapy dog on the outskirts of town for a much-needed break. Then her late sister's ex-boyfriend, Alec Wilkins, unexpectedly arrives with his toddler daughter, and this holiday refuge could become something more...

REDEEMING THE COWBOY
Stone River Ranch • by Lisa Jordan

After his rodeo career is ruined, cowboy Barrett Stone did not expect to be working with Piper Healy, his late best friend's wife, on his family's ranch. She blames him for her husband's death. Can he prove he's more than the reckless cowboy she used to know?

FINDING THEIR CHRISTMAS HOME
by Donna Gartshore

Returning home after years abroad, Jenny Powell is eager to spend the holidays with her grandmother at their family home. Then she discovers that old flame David Hart is staying there with his twin girls as well. Could it be the second chance that neither of them knew they needed?

THEIR SURPRISE SECOND CHANCE
by Lindi Peterson

Widower Adam Hawk is figuring out how to parent his young daughter when an old love, Nicole St. John, returns unexpectedly—with a fully grown child he never knew he had. Nicole needs his help guiding her troubled son. Can they work together for a second chance at family?

LOOK FOR THESE AND OTHER LOVE INSPIRED BOOKS WHEREVER BOOKS ARE SOLD, INCLUDING MOST BOOKSTORES, SUPERMARKETS, DISCOUNT STORES AND DRUGSTORES.

LICNM0823

HARLEQUIN
PLUS

Try the best multimedia subscription service for romance readers like you!

Read, Watch and Play.

Experience the easiest way to get the romance content you crave.

Start your **FREE TRIAL** at
<u>www.harlequinplus.com/freetrial</u>.